The Payback I Owe

Montesha Ford

Dedication ...

Oh my , words couldn't explain the praise I send to my Father GOD and his almighty angel that's been with me! I dedicate this book to first, my mother, Yvette Wells. I thought a lot about who I wanted to really mention in this and its her, my Queen. I love you, and pray you're blessed with nothing but the best in life. Second my big sister Terrisha Barr, my runner up in life as a princess. It was always difficult making your own name when your big sister was girly and attractive. To my sister I pray for your blessings the same. Next comes my beautiful daughter, reach for the STARS APRYL MAE!!!!!! Last but not least William Evans, someone I not known that long but encouraged me to finish this baby on up. I always wanted to be a novelist and short story writer but when this guy read my first few chapters and kept coming for more, it moved me. Jesus is with you all enjoy this book, and learn that family is who you make it, you always have a choice.

Table of Contents

The Intro

"Look ma'am, the evidence all points to YOU." The Detective slammed hard on the desk sitting in front of 25 year old, Cynthia 'Diddy' Meyers.

"the evidence COULD SPELL OUT MY DAMN NAME, IM NOT admitting to anything. Convict myself for what? I didn't even do anything. Y'all sitting here interrogating the wrong person while my man's killer is running freely. Who really does that though? Georgian police, fucking Frognat County crooked ass black people man. You probably one of them down low cops anyways sick bastard just want somebody to kiss yo ass. Na bruh, You aint getting a raise or none of that off me. I don't giv'a damn. Matter of fact where is my LAWYER?!" she spat in the ugly black officers face. With the time Cynthia had been spending in prison she was ready to unleash some anger on any cop, didn't matter the rank the color or the respect he was giving her. Rage was all she was seeing right now.

The officer wiped his face, his mug never changing, starring Cynthia dead in her eyes. He was feeling the heat and the tension between the two were beyond thick. The officer was getting real irritated with Diddy and her bad attitude. *Shes not getting off easy, I be damn I let this hoe fly. Why? so she can go out get another pimp and kill him?*

"Look, you sick bitch!" he was now yelling in her face at the top of his lungs. Cynthia was scared out of her mind; she'd been to jail a few times back in her home state but never in Georgia. Fleeing back to Portland Oregon with her daughter is where she was hand cuffed and arrested. It was mighty funny after finding her husband of 16 months dead in their home she even packed the little things she had and tried to leaving.

Nervous, scared, and gassy all at once, Cynthia was feeling low. She rolled her eyes to the back of her head trying not to cry and tilting her head back. Did she do something, why was she sweating out of fear if she didn't kill her husband? But the real question at hand is Why didn't this officer been call a lawyer when Cynthia requested one? how did he have the power to just grab her from her cell and question her. He wasn't even the officer to arrest her, some white bald guy by the name on his name tag read Smith did. How did the even get involved?

"You aint got to be yelling all in my face, I don't even fucking know what happen, I just got home and he was dead" Cynthia began crying she couldn't hold back the tears. Replaying the scene of her walking into her 3 bedroom condo and seeing things trashed. "you think I moved all the way here from my past to end up married to some pimp and kill him? I loved Ramone, he was my child's father what the fuck?!" she sobbed.

Chapter 1

January 13rd, 2016

It was 'bout 8:35 p.m. Saturday evening, Diddy was just leaving a regulars house she stopped by to deliver him some product no man could shake, PUSSY. Uno had her in the game and ever since then she couldn't shake the habit of giving a man 45 mins of her time for 550$, *most bitches don't even make this in a week.* She counted her money and folded it up placing it into her purse.

She was headed to get her daughter, sweet little Romney. So innocent to the world and didn't even have a clue what was going on in her parents life. She would soon though, everything that came up was bound to come crashing down, besides age of course. Romney had been spending most of her days when she was outside of school at one of Uno's 'employees' houses, Desire.

The way Uno had his women set up was like an assembly line, they all played an important part. If one didn't come through than everything went downhill so you know the whole operation of his business was based on TEAM WORK. Diddy pulled off slapping Futures new mixtape he had dropped not even an hour ago. dude stayed dropping mixtapes like it was the new crack no one mind though, his fans needed a hit of the new trap god around. Diddy rocked to the music dialing the girl Desire's number.

As soon as Desire answered all she heard was her daughters loud mouth just running, asking questions and rambling about school and her favorite cartoon character Doc Mcstuffin. "is that my mommy?" Desire rolled her eyes smiling. "No, yo mommy left you here with me forever!" she growled tickling the chubby little girl.

"Hey Desire, has she ate anything, im coming in like 15 minutes I'm right down the street." Diddy lied.

"bruh you was suppose to be hea' an hour ago. I got plays and shit calling my phone Diddy."

"Girl I said I was gone be a few if you was busy I wouldn't of dropped my baby off to you."

"now you know I love Romney." Desire said kissing romneys forehead and walking into the next room. "its just, We all aint have a baby by Uno and get wifed up you know." And that was nothing but the truth.

She think she just so better. I just don't get it though, we all helped get this shit to where its at. ;he wasn't the only one slanging dope and pussy. We all lost something to gain something and t wasn't even a huge gain, I could of did this shit on my own.

'Don't start that shit Desire foreal, all I got to do is make one fuckin phone call, you know not to lisrespect me in any kind of way." Diddy said turning down her music. Desire knew not to get mart, all 7 of Uno's employees knew who Diddy was. Besides being the mother of his first orn, she was the Madam to the Mister. Not everyone understood what that meant at first but fter marrying Uno they did. She was his ROCK, his SUN, his MOON, GOD had JESUS and Uno ad DIDDY.

sound like some hater shit." Diddy scoffed.

Oh my gosh if it wasn't for Uno I swea dis ho would be dead. High maintence wanna be ass itch, all because you helped Uno get his escorting service together, she act like she was foreal he brains. Desire smacked lips and straighten herself up as if diddy were standing in front of er. *All I got was a house, wasn't like he got me a house car sent me to beauty school like they romised years back.*

'look im sorry girl, I really am, I just gotta make a quick 1500 before Uno visits tonight, I got like more payments to give him and I officially own my house. When you called I was busy but I topped." She explained herself the best way she could without trying to offend diddy but the vay Diddy mind was set up she took everything the girls had to say to her offensive. "I been vatching your daughter all week like I think you really don't give a fuck. I cant be doing this shit o more diddy."

OH so you mad? Like bitch Don't be tryna blame my fucking child on your slip ups cause you ant keep your tricks in check, you aint on good terms where they spot you, like what the fuck ; you doing Desire? Falling in love? I send you more clients than any of the other btitches Uno ot, like seriously? You do hair and you fucking for money you should be making more than iamond." Diddy interrupted her yelling at the top of her lungs.

you being careless about the situation, you know Uno said no johns 'round dat baby so im especting his wishes."

what the fuck you mean DESIRE! Shes 4 you bet not have my baby around no tricks, I will slice a throat my damn self and im talkin in my uptown voice bitch you know its real. if any of them asty ass niggas look at my Romney its over with. " Diddy was petite, and Uno wasn't a big guy imself, but the way their daughter was built you couldn't tell. She was chubby yet, thick. Her thighs were solid, not baby fat. Her hips were a little wide, but Diddy made sure to put her on the right clothes so she looked her age.

"diddy whyre you talking to me like a bitch off the streets?" desires voice was cracking, she sounded like she wanted to cry, maybe because she was getting so fed up with the shit that Diddy and Uno put her through. Mainly Diddy because she was the voice. Diddy dropped Romney off 6 times this week already, and once was twice in one day. She was really being inconsiderate, knowing Desire had a job to do and if it wasn't done Uno'd have her ass beaten and taxed by all of them. It happened before but to a new girl they called Lindsay, you already know why. Bitch looked like Lindsay and partied even harder. With the first few thousand she got she did what any white bitch would do, surgery. Her boobs went from 36C's to 32DD's and she even got a butt lift. Uno had no problem with her upgrading herself it was the point of her OVER Spending on drugs to a point she overdosed on a few clients. You think Uno was having that? No fucking way, dude stomped her to sleep, checked her into the nearest emergency saying she was beaten and robbed. A week after being in the emergency they released her, and she doubled up the money by going to Italy and playing with the Italians. For some reason they were into red heads with freckles. But that wasn't the end of that, Uno also made her pay $350 a piece to all the women who handled her tricks when she was hospitalized.

"This is a fucking business! You miss out on money, they MISS OUT on money and you will fucking pay!" Uno bellowed. Making 4 of his girls who were standing in his reach flinch back. "stop fucking testing me and get this loot. We making fuckin moves, don't yall wanna stay lit?" he looked just like dude from paid in full. Sexy smile, white teeth, dark brown skin, but his hair was longer. It wasnt down his back or anything but he kept it long enough to show off the good hair he did have.

But back at Desire, who was so loyal to Uno and his come up that when Diddy called her, she stopped in the middle of getting 1200 from one of her undercover regulars visiting from Europe just to see her.

"Girl are you forgetting you was that bitch on the streets, I found? Not no fucking Uno. You was doing kitchen do's out yo mommas house. And you lucky I even did that because the bitches house is disgusting. You know I be so fucking tired of yall hoes acting like Uno really the one do all the work. Im here for yall hoes when yall need clothes, food, a place to stay he tell yall call me. I run the whole operation, I got keys to all the locks." She laughed to herself just thinking how she really bossed up. "He just the nigga on the infomercial, im the one making the moves I started this shit. And if you keep back talking me bitch ima show you why you should fear me and not that nigga Uno, have my fuckin daughter ready bye."

She threw her pink iPhone 5c down onto her custom pink 2016 volts wagon seat. She was so irritated she sped all the way there, and honked the horn when she was outside instead of going in and socializing like any old day.

Desire on the other hand, looked at her phone screen, "BITCH!" she screamed hanging up and looking to see if Romney had heard her. Seeing the coast was clear she spoke outloud to herself sitting down at her kitchen table rolling a joint. "Bitch promised me my own salon, my own house, my own whip, a fucking team that had me. They not my team, ima show this bitch. Just wait and see, fuck Uno too" She starred off into space hitting her joint. After a split second something came to mind. " Romney your moms outside." She yelled picking up her phone and dialing a number. Waiting for an answer she whispered to herself, "Ima get these mothafuckas for everything they owe me."

It was now 9:26 pm and Diddy was late, that 15 mins been flew by and her daughter, Romney had been waiting on the porch the whole time. "MOMMY!!" she screamed running toward the car.

"why are you outside baby come on." She opened the door from the inside. She watched her lil fatty girl wobble to the car and jump in. Desire had braided her hair into a beehive and the top was designed into a flower with beads hanging off. "your hairs so cute baby." She kissed her face and grabbed her chunky tummy.

"Auntie 'Sire did it." She touched it showing off Uno's smile. It made Diddys heart melt everytime seeing her favorite feature on Uno had passed down to their seed.

"Here, tell her thanks I appreciate it and youll be back soon." She counted out 120$ in 10's then sent her daughter to give it to Desire. *Bitch can do some hair.* She played in her 22 inch Peruvian bundles Desire also installed.

Moments later Desire popped out of the mint green 2 bedroom town house and into the door way, her slim thick figure waving and blowing kisses. She was so grateful for the money. Everytime. Being the girls hair dresser and an escort was so much on her. She shouldve been making at least 1000 more than the girls everytime since she did they hair into styles only celebrities would pay for but she was barely making the $200 more than them. All her money was going to the house she was paying Uno for under the table . diddy was the only one who really stunted when it came to money, just blowing it WHILE the others stayed on a limit giving her 60 70 bucks and a few I owe you's. *Bitch greener than this money* Desire thought to herself counting through it and watching Diddy as she peeled off.

" you remember daddys number don't you? call him." She told Romney, who was already playing in her phone. Diddy had been calling this man all day and the only response she was getting was the word *one* he had as his voicemail.

"no answer again mommy."

"what is your dad up to Romney." She asked looking at her daughter than back at the road.

"I don't know but he gone be in trouble." Romney giggled knowing her mom didn't play about that blowing up a nigga phone shit. *What the fuck is he doing that's so important he not answering his WIFES phone call, it could be anything like what if something was up with Rom'.*

She sped home, worried yet pissed all at the same time, "I know he bet not be with that bean and burrito ass Mexican Romney" she spoke aloud to her daughter. "I swear to GOD, im tired of arguing with him about this chick see men don't get it baby, you feed them clothe them bathe them spoil them and please all their needs just for you to be married than that's it? They think the marriage ceremony and the ring is the pay back but NO its not you suppose to return the favor all of it. I mean yeah im the boss but im not." She looked over at her daughter who was just starring at her blankly.

"whatre you talking about mommy?" she asked.

"nothing baby, mommy and daddy's business is all. We going to send you to a private school so you can get all the training you need so you can open up your own business too." She said grabbing her cheek and smiling.

"Mommy?"

"Yes baby" she answered.

"why do you call Marisol names? She doesn't call you names? She told me you were pretty" Romney admitted not knowing she had just pissed her mom off even more.

"Marisol?" she repeated in disgust, "who the fuck had you around her Romney?"

"Daddy said...." Romney started but stopped out of fear seeing her mother beat up her steering wheel. She sat there in silence thinking of the punishment her dad would give her for telling on him. He taught Romney never to snitch, even if it was to her mother.

Diddy pulled into an available parking spot.

"come on." Diddy said grabbing her daughter, purse, and keys all in that order. She walked into the building past the doorsman person and straight to the elevator. Romney pressed the #7 and they patiently waited to arrive onto their floor. Diddy was so much in a rage when she didn't hesitate opening the door she didn't even notice it was unlocked.

Stopping in an awe, she looked over the whole place being trashed maybe it was a robbery, but not many people knew where Diddy and Uno rested their head.

What the fuck! Diddy said to herself dropping everything, including her daughter who stumbled but landed on her feet "Romney go wait outside for mommy please." She said running toward the room where the money dope and stash of weed was. If it was a robbery they had to take the safe, but instead she found her husband. He was laid out onto the bed with a woman's face buried into his lap. DIDDY couldn't believe her eyes, he had the woman shed seen him with plenty of times sitting in his lap. The shocking part was, she was in their home, dead right along with his cheating ass, and Romney was right there behind her mother to witness it all. Shaking her head with tears filling her eyes Diddy covered romneys face. "what did you do?!" she yelled.

"I didn't do it mommy." Romney said burring her face into her moms leg.

"oh my lord, not you rom. Her!" she pointed to the dead body. walking up to it, She kicked it over to look at the bitch who had been creeping with her man. *The bitch is even prettier dead.*

"Come on baby." Diddy quickily thought of the routine Uno gave to her several times if anything had happen to him.

1. Get the kids
2. Get the money
3. Get the dope if you can.
4. Fly to Portland
5. Go to an address he'd writen down and deliver a package to some cat name 'DOS'

From that point on this 'DOS' cat would get Uno's operation back in to action.

"who the fuck is DOS?" diddy asked looking at the instructions Uno written down for her.

"Diddy." Uno looked into her eyes, "Ive done a lot of shit before you, and I done tried a lot of strategies crossed a lot of folks, but you my wife. I done brought you into a game only real men can play. But you a real woman, so I need you to just trust me. Im not asking nobody for forgiveness this is just what they deserve. And if something happens, I know they'll take care of you and Romney. I love you both." Cynthias eyes watered again as she grabbed the rest of her belongings leaving her husbands dead body along with his mistress. Before burning rubber trying to get off the scene she looked back at the building. *Damn baby, This shit was never apart of our plan.*

Scuuuuurrrrt. She peeled off.

Chapter 2

Cynthia 'Diddy' Franklin

It was back in 2008 I first met Uno, he had the cutest whitest smile ever. I mean teeth n pearl white status, fuck them golds, I wanted my man to have white straight teeth. Girls lways hollering about a nigga with golds in they mouth, like bitch what's under them golds hough? A rotten mouth, ugh that's the nastiest thing ever. Kissing and receiving head from a nan with brown crooked ass teeth. And I be damn if I ever date a GROWN man with braces. hat shit was so unattractive to me.

Ay name is Diddy for a reason. I was the BOOJIE of the BOOJIEST, didn't even have shit but vas nothing but high siddity. Coming from Portland Oregon I didn't have to tell people my ackground, they just knew I was a spoiled bitch. But not really. I just wanted better, so I ever stepped to a nigga or responded to a nigga who didn't have it. Yeah you blowing noney poppin bottles in the club, but what do you drive? Do you own it? Who do you live vith? Are you renting or paying mortgage? This type of shit mattered to me, because I was 17 enior graduate attending classes at PCC , smart as hell, grown as ever, adopted by rich half reeds who wanted me to be just like their daughter who was just like any regular light skin itch. I don't know how they would image me to come out like her when we were every bit of he opposite of each other. Growing up she got treated way better and it was fucked up ecause people at school, the park, and grocery store even seen it.

Ay black ass with this half breed family, didn't seem to really be working out in my favor. I nean even though they were black, they didn't act like it. They didn't talk like it, they didn't ress like it and they sure as hell didn't acknowledge it. Detra their only child, was about 3 ears older than me. We started at the same school, an all white science academy but I just ot kicked out because I couldnt tolerate all them damn white and Mexicans keep calling me igga boldly. I mean I let some of my friends slip up a few times and say it but show me some espect, like its years of slavery blood sweat tears and so much pain behind that word. I don't ee why people didnt get that these days, they didn't get it back in the 70's 80's & 90's so I uess they'll never get it right?

Ay hair was nappy but I definitely wasn't bald headed, people could call me skinny, chicken ead, Cinderella and more mean shit but they could never call me ugly or bald head. I night've been black too but I stayed getting questioned on what I was mixed with. I was a

good 5'4 124lbs, could never go over 126, I tried so many times, but like the folks in ga said that shit dead.

HONK! HONK! HONK! **I was too late to work leaving from school and this damn traffic was not helping.** ***HONK! HONK! OMG will this asshole get the fuck out of my way.***

My cell rang showing my bosses number, ***shit!*** **"Hey Martha, im really in a rush im on my way as we speak. Its really hard to talk and drive,"** ***Click.*** **I looked down at my phone and it was pitch black.** ***FUCK!!!!!!*** **Tears formed in my eyes, why is this day beating my ass. My hair already sweated out its wrap I had to put a nappy ass poof ball in the center of my head. My week old nail had broke, which was really a waste of money because it even the right paint I wanted. On top of that my job in the school store had just complained about how long they were, like this day couldn't get any worse. I haven't even smoked yet so I knew my day wasn't gone go right. Nobody was home, I couldn't call my foster sister Detra for some odd reason her phone was going to voicemail.**

"Aint no reason a pretty lady like you should be tearing up out of frustration." An old school box chevy appeared on the drivers side of my 2006 honda, I bought for 1000 at the auction on 148thsandy. It startled me and I almost screamed, "Could you not play with me right now. Im late for work and my phone just died on my boss. Im just so…" I exhaled deeply, it kind of helped or maybe it was the smile on the man that I was now eyeing.

"where you headed I got connects." He asked throwing both hands up. "shit, I might even say fuck it and take care of yo pretty self. You real pretty in that car, what you look like when you out of it?" traffic still wasn't moving, why the hell didn't I just get off the E way on 60th.

"you aint finna do shit." I said rolling up my window and my eyes. It really wasn't him, it was the heat. It was an irregular 104' degrees, Portland aint never been this hot. Global warming must be really be real. The air in my car was sho'll tripping too. He smiled and waved me off, "missing out on something real." The lane he was in was now moving and so was he. Late another 30 mins, for no indefinite reason. Thats my ass, I'm finna be jobless.

"Im so sorry James, there was alot of traffic and my teacher was giving this big assignment" I started walking up to my bosses son who was still my boss. As soon as I spotted his tall lanky white self i knew to run to him and not his momma. James was a student right along aside my foster sister Detra at PSU. He sweated Detra so much, some days hed do her homework so

shed have time to spend with him. Ha I guess, so me being smart I figured since his mother is the owner, I could get the hook up. Which I did, kinda, if you ask me shit could of went smoother but it didn't. I worked at a local home depot off 102nd a few blocks south of stark.

"Cynthia, manners, please. " James demanded as I approached him and a familiar face.

"Oh my god, really?" I rolled my eyes looking away than turning back to the dude who was driving the box chevy I had come upon earlier. James cleared his throat.

"This is a friend of my dad's down at the Bureau." He said licking his thin pink lips.

"my apologies James." I quickly apologized for being late, at least I thought that's what I was apologizing for.it was kind of awkward at that second, I was looking Mr Do-you-look-good-outside-the-car up and down and just as he was giving me the same look. James on the other hand was looking us back and forth standing there, but nobody spoke.

"so you must be a cop?" I asked looking at James than back at whatever his name was.

Than he smiled, ooh that smile was lovely as fuck.

"No. " he put his hands in his pocket, "Matter of fact, Im here for some supplies yo dad told me come and pick up." He pulled out a short list and handed them off to James. James was still standing there, im surprised he didn't been check me about being late for the cameras than say sorry later. He was funny like that, be mean than apologize like he needed friends. He was the manager and going to school for law, aint no way In hell I needed him when I had Detra. She was going to be a Lawyer, but she had James and he was just months away from graduating, he was that kind of smart that he could go to the feds after college.

James looked it over and handed me the list "Go get these things in the back for him, ring it up but scan it under sampled." James thought he was slick, his daddy too. Stealing from the damn store, but I guess it aint stealing if yo mom or wife owns the place huh, ha I heard that. I nodded my head taking the list from his cold pink hands and walking off hoping this dude knew to follow behind me. He did.

"so, James daddy a crooked ass cop, I knew it." I admitted looking back at him.

He was smiling real hard this time, "yep I fucking knew it. I mean why else would he associate with a black guy who looks like a pimp? You got too much going on to be a pimp, plus you in a chevy you a drug dealer?" I was straight stereotyping dude, but he didn't have a problem with it. To be honest he never said no so I believed James father, Officer Sir'Gimes, weird ass name, was dirty.

I carried the things to the counter and rung them up just how James instructed me. "Yall killed somebody didn't yall?" I asked curious looking over the things he had purchased.

"You smart as hell aint you? You got it all figured out." He said throwing his hands up again and laughing to himself. "put it to use and let a nigga get with you."

"you think you cute." I said rolling my eyes, I hated when niggas from the west coast did that shit. Thinking they cute.

Chapter 3

"Cynthia, so your telling me you didn't know you had chlamydia for the 5th time before entering here?" he asked with seriousness in his eyes. The ugly black cop looked like a cross between forest whitaker and terry crews, no offense but a man that buff and intimidating should be in the army serving his country the right way. Not interrogating me, I'm innocent.

"5th time?" I repeated.

"Yeah 5th time, your medical records indicate you haven't gotten it since April 2010,right before giving birth to your child. That's when you stopped working right? Before giving birth to your bastard child? Than it looks like here.." he reached into a bag pulled a file and read quickily turning back to me , "you stopped escorting but caught the shit again so either your husband was creeping or your still working?" I shook my head. This shit was ultra crazy, medical records are supposed to be discreet, confidential, fucking private. "WHO THE FUCK is you to pull my medical records? And my daughter isn't a bastard." I scoffed.

"You don't get it do you? Mrs. Meyers, I know you and your whole family, especially your husband, iknow him personally." He said throwing down his file, which looked like a dictionary.

"you don't know shit." I snapped.

"I know enough to know hes into shipping women like you across the fucking globe for money. You being the mother of his child, a girl. a fucking girl, you want your daughter growing up in this type of shit." I understood him, I understood him very clear. The point was I WASN'T here about my fucking daughter and or my living situation.

"the IRS has been up this mans ass, and you're his wife you don't think their coming for you, FBI will be here shortly but I plan on making my case before that."

"my husband was killed, murdered by a jealous mothafucka hating in these Georgia streets go find them."

"You know weve all been watching him for A long time now Cynthia, I personally been watching him. I watched him recruit a lot of you." I wiped the sweat off my brow, and grabbed at my wrist they were aching like hell in these cuffs. I was so clueless but in the back of my mind and inside my gut something told me Uno had this shit coming.

"Feeling guilty for something over there? I have one of your ladies in custody, someone ready to talk. Cynthia I plan on taking down your whole operation and booking you with all 3 of the murders." He said so sure he had me for something, looking me dead in the eyes.

"I don't know what the fuck is going on, it was 2 murders now 3?"I shook my head again wanting to cry. He was just hyping me up.

"when you ready to talk and tell me what you have going on as a whole im here." He said reaching for a hand. "what the fuck is the hand gesture for, support? Yall locked me up In front of my child!"

"It wouldn't be the 1st time." His nostrils flared. "Do you like being a whore?" he asked twitching a little. I ignored his question and took a deep breath. "I asked you a fucking question, do you like being a whore?"

"its not a profession."

"So you say."

"someone killed my husband and, when I come out innocent I want police protection, they'll come for me next." I was really trying to throw him off the topic but it made sense. If they killed him and his bitch, than they had to know about me. They have to know about Romney.

"Who?" he asked intrigued on what id say next.

"My husband wasn't always true to me and I knew that but I don't necessarily know what he did but I know it has something to do with clientel."

"Ahhhhhh." The man smiled, "so your not as dumb as you acting." He clapped.

"I wasn't apart of an operation, we were poor lovers trying to come up, I got pregnant and we decided to go square." I lied my hardest trying to get him to go look for this killer.

I knew Ramone had connections tho. He was hiding something from me but he kept this secret hidden deep. He was connected to the feds as you can see, he probably knew this mark ass nigga. But he wasn't the only one with connections either. See Ramone thought Detra was just James little ghetto ass girlfriend, but she wasn't. Ramone obviously wasn't that much into detail, like isaid something told me he was getting what he deserved. It had to be he hid in the shadows of everything too much. Now looking back on it I let him drag me into all this shit. If I could take it back, I believe id ride even harder for this man tho. He was the only one there, just ke I know hes the only one here now. I can feel him, its just weird hed leave me to be blamed or his murder. I hated him sometimes but id never kill him.

My look out was my sister Detra, I had her scoping the scenes of every move me and Uno nade together before we all got involved as a team, and even after we got together I paid her o still look out. I loved my man but I loved my money more and in order to keep the money I ad to keep the man, in my sight that is.

girl I don't know I don't trust this guy Uno, he kinda shady." Detra said swinging her honey londe hair. She had dyed it to where it was matching her skin tone. The foster sister n out ven more ghetto than me. Nails long, and weave even longer, true stripper look going ompletely on, but the bitch never even thought of dancing. Hoe came from money, momma doctor daddy a lawyer. Youd think shed want to follow in her mothers footsteps but shed ay all her time would be taken so she wanted to follow in daddy's shoes.

Really Detra, just look out for me if I don't get more than 5,000 tonight I swear im not doing no more." I explained to her unbuckling the seat belt to her gray audi, "5,000 to do what ho Diddy?!"

it's a private party De', ima dance, keep the money from that and once I spot dude he ooking for get him in a room alone, you know freak em a little." I did a dance motion, "But vith clothes on and Uno gone come in and rob em, it's a perfect plan." I flapped my hand like was nothing. Shit I was down for Uno he had me ready to go.

Okay DIDDY howre you gonna make this happen though, what if he don't wanna go in a oom with you?" she was just concerned and I could understand that but hearing this hoe run er mouth was irritating my life at the moment.

why you acting like I aint paying you?" I asked rolling my eyes.

I cant be concerned about my fucking best friend?"

best friend??? Bitch im yo sister! Wit yo jealous ass"

Jealous? Fuck I need to be jealous of I been getting money." ***and gladly taking the money I een giving you .***

you starting to sound like a hater to me, Its 5 racks damn, ima take us out when I get it, if is nigga serious about some money than im with it. I aint got a family like you I gotta get ines the way iget it." I opened the car door stepping out in the red bottoms Uno had bought e. He'd known me a solid week and was telling me how ready we was to put money in my

pocket. I don't know if that was some west coast shit or love was rreally feeling me. But I loved it, no more broke ass Lloyd center shopping, I was downtown at pioneer square, in Washington, woodburn at outlets, we even drove to seattle and salem just to buy one or two outfits for a night in vegas. He had me feeling real right and if Detra was jealous I could see why, my little ghetto ass had come up on a lick.

"my family took you in a long time ago Diddy , your like my sister and I love you. Don't let this getting money shit fuck up your school work and you fall in love with his money." She wasnt lying, her mom and dad I guess were just too busy for an only child and adopted me. Who knows who my mom is or was. She might be dead so no shade thrown against her, she probably was homeless and did what was best for me.

"for your family to have loved me so much, they still treated you better." I said slamming the door and storming off. I hate when mothafuckas want a thank you for something they didn't do. That job I had back in home depot, I had to literally stalk James for it I mean yeah she put in the word but I STILL had to get myself in. James mom was a total bitch, she didn't call me back until after a month. Not to mention Detra college tuition was paid in full for the 8 years she planned on attending school. Me? Mines? Oh I had to look toward financial aid and a scholar ship. I still never got the chance to see what college was about with sororities and stressing over a dorm room or anything like that. Community college was where I was and I was stuck there until I met Uno.

"Cynthia." The officer stroked his temples.

"Look, ill tell you what I know." I said wiping my tears.

"Go head." He reached in his pockets pulling out a tape recorder.

"A tape recorder? That's the best you can do, its 2016." I scoffed.

"Shut yo snitch ass up and speak into the damn recorder, last time I checked you had an iphone 5c them damn things aren't even reliable." He finished setting it up and waited for me to speak

I looked at him with so much hate and disgust, I just wanted to hawk a huge ass loogie in his eyes.

"I met Ramone Uno Meyers back in 08, I was always in it for the love. So he kept shit hidden from me..."

"WE DON'T WANT TO HEAR THIS BULLSHIT, you don't get your facing the death penalty?! 3 murders" he held up 3 fingers.

“3?” I repeated clueless.

“3! Yes, the woman, your man, and the unborn child.”

“UNBORN CHILD?” my heart damn near stopped.

“She was 8 weeks pregnant Cynthia, you didn’t know that?” he knew that shit was eating me alive. I couldn’t even cry that shit he just said got my blood boiling. “got anything you wanna admit to, anything you wanna say?” he smirked.

August 12th 2013

I was 7 months pregnant with Romney and she was kicking my ass. It wasn’t a hot day In Oregon but the more we faded off into the clouds I was sweating my neck off.Romney must of knew mommy was just as scared as she was because I damn near threw up. It wasn’t my first time it was just my first time pregnant and i was just so cautious of things that would affect Romney. Flying pregnant, was that legal? I looked out the window, Italy here we come. I sat back closing my eyes, I could feel air from the vent above me, when I open my eyes it was Uno adjusting the air. “this gone be so fun”.

“No, its not, Lindsay gotta get that money back. You gotta meet the new girls James has to come with me. I just wish he didn’t bring detra.” He spoke under his breath.

“shes gonna be like my midwife or something why you worried about her?”

“she not making nobody no money.” He looked at me like I was dumb. “fuck you mean why im worried about her. Who is the bitch, is she fucking him? Why is you taking care of her if he is?”

“if im touching bread so is my sister.” I said getting out of my seat, “Move.” I brushed passed him and to the bathroom. I took a few deep breaths and washed my face. this fucking pregnancy was seriously dawning on me. I was so fat.

When I made my way back to my seat it was a Mexican looking bitch all smiled up in my man face. He didn’t pay me no mind, just continued chatting it up. I let him get that, yeah flirt with the bitch if you want, thatd be coming out of his pockets.

She was about 5’6” slim but curvy in a way, big light blue with a hint of hazel eyes. Her hair was thick and dark black the bitch really looked like a Kardashian, and I sure did peep her. I peeped everything on her from her powder soft gel pink toe nail polish to her diamond stud

earrings that probably costed 920 on sale from Kays. She was wearing toe out silver red bottoms I wanted that had just got released but my foot was too fucking fat.

I scooted pass the two rolling my eyes and pushing my big belly into unos face. He pulled back making a face but continuing his conversation.

"that's my baby moms, but she know im a business man." He smiled at her.

"Oh really, hi mami, Im Marisol, im on my way to Italy."

"no shit." I said looking out the window, I wasn't finna meet this bitch. Im not friendly but I guess this nigga was, we didn't need anymore females we had 2 waiting in Italy the fuck did we need her for? Like seriously though. He had me to talk to anyways.

A few days into the trip, I seen the same Mexican bitch in our hotels, the same resturants, I even seen the bitch back in the US. But this time, in photos with Uno. Wow, I couldn't believe he was creeping with a bitch dead in my face but really while I was pregnant. He didn't like Detra because he ran into her every time he was doing dirt and knew she would be the one to tell me. I thought that shit was behind us, I at least thought after confronting him hed give her up. But he didn't, he kept this bitch around for a long time. Even after marrying me, the bitch was at our wedding with gifts. I couldn't stand her. I couldn't stand him.

Chapter 4

You couldn't pay me to snitch. I been sitting here for 2 weeks as it is, Im not scared. Im not nervous, im hella mad YES. Glad the baby was dead but then again that's fucked up because I wouldn't wish death on nobody but the pussy niggas in this world who deserved it. Like that dick who was rich as ever and wanted to run for president just to do it. Sad.

"Ramone was my love, yes I used to work in the sex trade game, that I am guilty of. I will admit to being a bad mom because after having Romney I was still working. But I stopped after he married me last year and that's on his grave."

"your lying Cynthia." He interrupted me.

"how the fuck you know, you not me." I itched my nappy fro.

"you really wanna try me?" he asked reaching under the table. I watched his every move, leaning over when he did.

When he rose he threw the pictures of me and a couple johns ive seen over the last few weeks.

"so yall got this shit planned out don't yall? Who sent you?" I asked bluntly standing up.

"Guard, Guard." I called. No one responded, the officer didn't even move.

"Im above every officer in this building. Ill see you again Cynthia. And youll tell me everything I want to know. With James, with the money, and those girls."

"GUARD!!!" I screamed banging on the door. This guy was creeping me out, and the last thing I really needed was a federal agent scooping into my files bringing up more charges.

"the only thing you can do for me is make sure Detra gets my baby girl."

"naw, ima ride this one out, I want to see the outcome." He was now talking into my right ear. He reached over me and knocked lightly onto the door, "Im done." The door opened letting it air and bright lights.

I was damn ready to get back to my cell. I sure was. I needed to be alone, but I also needed to use the phone.

"can I call my sister?" I asked the bailiff that was escorting me back.

“just because you look good in orange.” He smiled and grabbed my forearm leading me toward the phones.

I dialed her number nervously, I really hoped shed answer. Since the first day I was brought in she ignored me.

“why do you keep calling me?” she finally answered.

“I need you to get Romney Detra please, for me.”

“im not doing shit for you. I moved to Georgia for you. I watched out for you, I rode for you and you didn’t listen huh?” she scoffed.

“you told me not to fall in love with the money and I didn’t. I fell in love with him Detra and I swear on Romneys life I didn’t kill him. I love him, after all this shit I still love him and would do anything to see him again.”

“this man has ruined you. he gave you a daughter at an early age, turning tricks, dropping out of school, he even gave you a disease.”

“that’s not a proven fact, look theres something going on Detra and im scared.”

“oh now you scared, I been scared CYNTHIA , Romney is probably fucking scared.” She hollered.

“this case has gone federal De’ their going to kill me.” I sobbed. “they are going to lock me away from some shit I didn’t do and my daughter has to suffer. How the hell you think I feel?!” I said pounding on my chest. “im worse than my mom at least she had the decency to hide her self from the shame, im all out with it. Asking you for a helping hand as my sister. I can easily call one of the girls but I trust you.”

“ive done all I can do, as much as I love my Rom-Rom, im weeks from becoming a lawyer, maybe after getting hired I can help you but as if right now. I can’t risk associating with you. You’re a dead woman walking, and itd be a juicy case but I cant.”

“why tf not? Ive been there for you.”

“because I think you’re the reason James was killed.”

Click.

My heart fucking dropped. I had no one, nobody, I couldn’t even get in touch with Romney.

“Damn that sucks.” The balliff looked me in my face expecting a reaction, I just hung the phone
p and walked with the man toward my cell.

Chapter 5

DeAytra Franklin

I hung the phone up on my fuck up of a sister. How could she put me in this shit when I was so close to achieving my dreams? My eyes were getting heavy but I wasn't going to cry I was just going to write it out. Yeah write James another love letter he would not receive because he was 6 feet under. He was dead, he was gone and I couldn't help. I wasn't there and I don't care if it was Uno's fault. She brought me into it, I didn't expect to get kidnapped and the only person who came for me was James. In a rage shooting everywhere, sadly I got away and he didn't make it out. The last 2 hours we spent together in that damn warehouse was everything though. Little did anyone know I was going to have his baby, id been waiting for the perfect time to have it and right now happiness awaits me.

DEAR James,

James, my sweet james. If I could Take it all BACK BABY I would. Id kiss those pink thin lips, I miss the taste it was like like a pink starburst. You know people sweat those, I don't really like em, but I had to compare them lips to something everyone likes. Im so so so sorry I should have been more careful I should of listen to you and just quit after I got the house. You always told me to do what was best for me and I was being greedy. James, please, come back . ive never prayed so much, ive never loved someone before and I didn't expect for it to be this way. We should be doing everything somewhere working, no like really working, you a FBI agent and me your wife, the lawyer. We went perfectly tgether. I miss the white off you. Remember that night we made love? So beautiful, I had just got into a fight with diddy I was feeling so low, body was hurting mind was even worse, but you made me feel alright, ran my bath water, wiped the tears out my eyes. We smoked our first joint even got drunk, off box wine . awhh man I miss you. So much....

Tears flowed onto the paper and I couldn't stop smiling, it was love. This love was so real, and I fucked it up. I let my greed and loyalty to my foster sister fuck my life up. I don't blame her I don't blame me I don't even blame james I blame my mother. She adopted Diddy all because she didn't want to deal with me, she rather been in the hospital dealing with strangers who probably didn't do anything but shit and complain. Something her child at home would've did for years. But thts fine , she can do what she wants now. It seems like since I left she calls me more, practically begging for my attention. To be hinest, im not going to even entertain her.

Looking over my love letter, only wanted to make me think of revenge, like who could I retaliate my mans death on. Whose life or lives would I just destroy. i was sitting at my desk In my 4 bedroom home Diddy bought me a few years back. Yes, business we beyond booming. Diddy made Uno's dreams come true with all the money, dope, and traveling they were doing. James was murdered because I was being dumb.

I had a 4 bedroom with no one to live with me, no one to come home and yell, "honey Im home." No one to rub my feet no one to make dinner for. My life was all planned out when I was running with diddy. James and I was getting in and getting out who knew pussy would really bring us this far. We robbed a couple drug lords, set em up, but it still was beyond them buyin the women we had to offer. The statement Pussy ruled the world was correct, I mean half of them girls were worn out in a way. Like Diamond, we found her in the strip club, she was pretty, a bartender. But she wasn't making any real money without being naked. Not to mention her drinks had too much alcohol to the point you didn't need a secondary drink. So she was turning tricks in the back, 40 50 bucks for a hand job. Diddy found out about her when Uno had her in the strip joint to catch a fish. Diamond is low class, I heard them saying it a lot, she was a pretty face, but she was too easy and influenced. Why have a broad like that on your team?

"because, shes willing." I heard Unos voice play in my head. I rolled my eyes, why would I even think about such an asshole. He didn't love my sister, and if he did he wouldn't of left her the way he did, matter of a fact he wouldn't of been off cheating with the Mexican girl I caught him with so many times.

Like that right there is why you should never trust a pimp. He married Diddy, had a child, and still cheated. Throughout the whole thing tho, the woman even showed up to their wedding, with gifts trying so hard to be with Uno. Im thinking maybe she seen money and went for it. Maybe she wanted what Diddy had. And if you wanted that you wanted to be used and then thrown on the shelf as a trophy. Diddy thought it was so cool to be a wife of a hustler, but didn't think about what would happen if all this shit ended. All over women, and greed. Like these Russians, Europeans, Italians, Mexicans, even the Asians cared for women. Not women from off the streets or in their neighborhood, but the illegal women. The women they had to pay for, it's like rich people love testing out breaking the law just to see if they can and if you ask me they cant. Not while im on the stand representing them.

Just put it this way, im not here for the people who break laws, im here for the innocent who really need my help. I thought diddy needed me, but in reality she was using me. And its real crazy because I knew it, james told me.

With everything going on, and happening so fast I was really confused on my next move. James didn't have a proper funeral because his body was into pieces. They didn't kill him just a shot to the head, but chopped him into pieces and spread him out so that we would HAVE to look for him.

The message was clear, whoever the fuck kidnapped me was beefing with Uno. I don't think Diddy made any enemies, and if she did it made sense they came after me since she didn't really have a bloodline to go after.

The first name that came to mind was a dude I knew she had set up a while ago, but last I heard he was in jail. All the men, they set up usually went to jail. That's all I needed to find out was who did this, why they did it and get they ass for it. It was simple sounding, but without James I barely had access to files that I needed. My first file would be on Uno, who was this Uno, really. Where did he come from, what did he come from, and what was he really going for. It had to be something bigger than this. Why else would it just be this, we didn't go international for it to just be this.

I got back up and logged into my computer signing into James FBI account. I'm pretty sure someone would see I accessed his things since he was deceased and the FBI navigated every device that was connected to them.

I typed in Uno, and nothing came up. I typed in his full name, Ramone Meyers, no Ramone but Romel Meyers. Romel Meyers, 6'4 209 lbs, gray eyes, tattoos and a birth mark on his right eye just under his eyebrow. No children, no wife, one family member popped up and it happen to just say a brother. No name, not a picture, not one single thing about this brother. Uno's real name was Ramone, not Romel.

So I searched under Cynthia Meyers and everything about her popped up to her real parents, to me and my family, to the one she has now. Her, her daughter and husband, it even included some of the girls she had working under her. The files read shed been apart of a huge wanted list behind Uno. Her alias was under Diddy Girl, all her arrest, all her jobs shes ever worked, medical records, schooling information and all was on there. After printing everything, I spread it out onto my bed ready to investigate what was going on here.

Romel Meyers, a brother? The man in the picture looked just like Uno when I held there pictures together, but he wasn't him. I really couldn't tell if it was him or not, but It said under the man's mug shot hed been released a few months prior to today's date which doesn't add up. Either Uno has been living a double life, or this man in this photo is indeed a twin. I looked up a current address, it said he was back in Portland Oregon living in a half-way house, but this wasn't any regular half way house. This one was secluded. Looking through more paper work I found A number he could be reached at. Im so determined to find out everything, if this is the first step im taking it. I quickily picked up my phone dialing *67 blocking the call.

"Hello?" a scratchy female voice answered. It was low and sounded as if she had a mic to her throat, you know one of them people whose probably had lung cancer.

"Hi hello, im looking for a Romel Meyers? Does he still stay there?" I asked in my sweetest yet educated voice.

"Who wants to know?" she asked intrigued.

I cleared my voice trying to find something to say real quick, but she interrupted me, "Hes not in so if this is his probation officer, he told me to tell you hes at work."

"Okay, okay, do you know when hell be in?"

There was a small silence, "What did you say your name was?" this lady was really onto me wasn't she?

"This is Cynthia." I lied. "im his sister in law, I married his brother, I believe I did. He has a twin right?"

"are you asking me about your brother? You seem so unsure baby?" she had to be older, because this woman was beyond nosy.

“He’s my brother in-law ma’am, actually I was on my way to Portland and wanted to make sure he was still living there.” I looked over the picture of the house he was staying in. it was a big brown dingy looking color probably a 5 bedroom looking at how huge it was with a two door garage.

“Oh okay, Cynthia. Ill let him know you called, it says your calling all the way from Georgia, you in Georgia?” it sounded as if she was trying to figure out if I was lying or not.

“Oh no maam, no, I actually am on my way, im on a bus I should be there shortly. Im using a total strangers phone. I don’t know much about Sevon, but I figured since I had his niece.”

“he never talked about a family, itll be great to see you. Well baby im going to finish making this dinner. Ill see you soon, id tell Sev too call you back but.”

“if he can.” I added.

“oh I thought you said you were using a strangers phone?”

I laughed nervously, “You know what ma’am you are right, he doesn’t want to call this number back unless he wants to talk to a complete stranger. So ill just seen him soon.”

“Okay baby.” She hung up and I let out a deep breath. Sheesh. I have to get used to this lying stuff if I was going to figure out what was going on and stay on top of these lies. I couldn’t afford to get caught.

I googled the next flight out to Portland. Im too determined, I found out Uno had a twin brother. What the hell?

Chapter 6

Who is Uno

Im up next, why? because I'm that nigga. I did a lot of dirt to get where im at and I be damn if any bitch or nigga tries to take me down. Met my baby moms and got a come up. I mean shit, she was young and ready. You gotta go for the young ones that's finna be legal and look good. She can be a 6 & after im done with her shes a solid 10, just off confidence though. I aint with that ice all my hoes out type shit. She got the dough just like I did. I had that bitch robbing, stripping and hoing. It was a choice, I mean shit shorty didn't have shit. but I love that girl to the bone of me. She put me on with a lot of bitches. I mean I had the connects with niggas as it is because my bro who locked up but that's some other shit but my bro all his clientele are all mines stupid ass nigga thought I was too young for the family business. Like nigga please im up next! He might've been thugging before me, but fuck all that, when I told that nigga I was ready he should of put li'l bro on. Instead he was on some selfish shit, wanted to be like Scarface, but didn't have a solid team. Than when I told him about getting this money with these hoes he questioned my intelligence like, did I ever plan on having kids because drugs were one thing but selling pussy with these young bitches were another? But iont give a fuck, enough about that nigga he out the way now and that's all that matters. It aint like I killed him, shit he deserved to be out my way. Nigga was tripping over an older bitch and her daughter. If the hoe wanted to get down for me at the age of 15 that's her you feel me, we family aint no need in touching me, I understand everything. But like I said that's some other shit and the only thing I'm here to do is tell my story.

Met my baby moms back in 08, excuse me she more than my baby moms, that's my damn wife. I aint no sucka, and I aint no duck, I just had a bitch that was down for me and decided to keep her. With all the dishonor and bullshit I had going on I needed to find me a little go'er and leave Portland fast. my bm's was like everything to me, she was sexy, smart, slim, thick in the right places but most of all dog she was high maintence in a way. She liked finer things because she never had it and I told her if she put her mind to it she could do it. Just thinking about the bitch got me going. Her sister who wasn't even her real fucking sister was jealous. She had a nerdy white boyfriend who pops work as an officer who I used to exchange a lil something for a lil nothing. A favor for a favor, he was taking the glory home from busting big drug deals, while I take the money and run. Of course I hooked the deals up, set these niggas up but who gives a fuck, im shiesty like that im a shady ass nigga tryna get paid, if my momma wont gimme 10 dollas ima take that shit so that should explain my character better than anything. Im a nigga wholl have beef withcha and take that shit beyond cow. Ima real nigga if you ask me, im what these movies portray to be.

im looking up at her now because I didn't go to heaven. They made like hell was horrible and I don't even think I was bad enough to make it there. Im stuck in my grave, cold wet mud under me. Damn shit was ruining my blood red cashmere suit. I got it made for a special occasion, and never got to wear it. Who would f thought I would be wearing to my own funeral. Ahhhh that's some shit, I guess this is the suffering for ALL ne bad I did. My first week here I was bugging, going insane, yelling for everyone I even thought somebody uried me alive. Naw, I was wrong, a few days ago I realized I haven't died. I wasn't hungry, I wasn't thirsty, I idn't sleep, I didn't even think. Everything I said, I said aloud to myself. Me thinking right now aint even me ninking, its me talking to myself. Man this shit here hell foreal. Ive always liked to hear myself talk but now, I ıst wanna shut the hell up and beg for forgiveness. I rather actually be in front of the devil. Maybe that was , I was the devil. This is what the hell I got for fucking up people's lives.

ooking over my daughter Romney she was so beautiful. Questioning everyone where I was where her nother was where desire was where anyone who shed remember was, the next kin was my brother but he idn't know about her, plus the bitch nigga wouldn't want her anyway. Who knows what he would do to my aughter if he knew about her existence. I wasn't that much of a savage I still had a heart, it was for Diddy ut diddy wasn't blood. Then again I treated my blood like shit when he was down. And now that hes out, nd im dead not even being abled to see the face of my murderer was haunting me and I wasn't gone rest in eace until someone helped me.

o I focused everything on Diddy, hoping wishing praying shed get out and be proven innocent. Yes I was heating with the Mexican girl but she knew that. Ima fucking pimp of course I test out all my hoes ventually, but this woman, Marisol. She was different, she was diddy in my eyes just a different culture. She as smart, she had everything diddy had but me, so why not share the wealth. I mean I wasn't tricking herever I went she could afford it, what ever I wanted she could get me. I mean what side bitch you know now up to the wedding with gifts, YES gifts. She didn't have kids and that just turned me all the on. I don't now, it was just something about her. She was dangerous in a way, she loved being in public with me, she as willing to deal with diddy and her bullshit. But she kept it so classy, and I loved her. And the day we got urdered was the day I found out about me being her childs father. I was gone be her 1st baby dad, I don't now what was so special about being the 1st but I was excited. I was happy, you know when I was shot, I ctually lived for another hour. Bleeding out slowly, sad crying. Yes a nigga was crying screaming.

was just told I was going to be a father than all of a sudden a mothafucka pops out shooting. Who the fuck id it though. I don't even care why, I know why, I HAD BITCHES trained to go, I had the dope game on lock. I as doing international deals, and whatever happen with James was just a minor set back. I gave his dad a ouple stacks. It wasn't like I left the nigga dead. I told his ass let her be. They wasn't gone kill that bitch etra. She was fine yeah, she was his bitch yeah. But she wasn't finna fuck all my shit up because she was a osy bitch out here snapping pictures writing down license plates and shit like a detective ol messy ass bitch. ne was the reason one of my best soldiers was down

Chapter 7

Cynthia Meyers

That bitch Detra wasn't shit! How could you say you love my baby, you love me we family and not take her in? all the money I spent with this burnt out scandalous fake ass lawyer bitch! Yeah that's exactly how I feel. This bitch was fake, probably killed uno how jealous her fagget ass was.

"LIKE REALLY!" I shouted out loud hitting my fist against the concrete wall.

"hey you keep acting crazy shouting and shit ima come in there!" a guard from down the hall yelled.

"FUCK YOU you fuckin pig." I screamed back running up to the gate. I heard foot steps coming my way but how I really was feeling like really really feeling. Fuck this pig, fuck this sentence, fuck these bitches, fuck this system. I fell victim to it and no one really gave a fuck. No one, the only real one I had on my team was uno and now im alone. Don't even have my daughter, hadn't seen her in weeks. Who knew where she was or what she was doing. What if she was living with some perverted people? Or just in a fucked up home? What if she was somewhere better and never wanted to come back home with her mommy? What if I never get out to see my baby?

BOOP

The fuck?! I rubbed the right side of my face, I had flew into the wall from a blow that was probably from the officer id called a pig. "You can't fucking do that!" I screamed and he grabbed my throat.

"I told you shut the fuck up. You wanna disrespect me, Ima show you." I was dead ass in a choke hold. What type of shit really was this? I was struggling, on my way to passing out.

"You .... Gone ... kill .... Me." I was reaching over my head scratching at his face. He finally released me when I got skin deep.

"Ahh." He grabbed at his right eye in agony. "Bitch" he kicked me to the ground. I was trying to catch my breath and make it to the other side of my little ass box of a cell.

"HELP!" I yelled. "HELP ME!" I was coughing and hoarse. "SOMEBODY! PLEASE HES TRYING TO KILL ME!" he snatched me up by my hair jerking my neck; I heard it crack. Than splat, I flew face first into the wall. My life was going so down drain so quick. I went from boss ass bitch to jail bird ass bitch. Wow. I couldn't see my baby, my husband was dead, and my sister cut me off, and the only people I could call on now was GOD.

“GOD.” I whispered. Boom, a left jab, “Please” I winced at the pain grabbing my side. Boom another in my stomach. That one was the one that one took me down.

I woke up in just my bra and panties, the cell was a little bit bigger but this time there was a metal cold ass bed with just a blanket. SERIOUSLY! I hopped up trying to ram the door like a fucking lunatic. I knew damn well I wasn’t getting out of here and I knew damn well where I was. I was in the got damn hole. My body was aching, I could feel my tummy turning. I just dropped to my knees and prayed. I prayed harder than ever. GOD if you hear me please please please, keep my daughter save. Aint no hope for me.

Detra Franklins

The next 18 hrs

It was 12 noon and this damn plane couldn’t land soon fast enough. I was ready to at least go to my room and sleep, but I could just stop by and see if hes there at least before I got settled in. It would be dumb as hell for me to pass it up when its on the way right?

It was these loud white children looked to be about 2, and the other about 4 arguing and fighting. The mother and father totally ignored the two screaming and going at it I just kept thinking of me and James conversation about children who acted out in public.

“Oh hell naw, see that type of stuff right there get you spanked.” I said glaring at the woman who was dragging her child across the marble mall floor we were visiting the great paris where shopping was perfect for. Really we were on a mission to bust these French men who smuggled American women and rob them for their cliental and money. If they had drugs it was extra for what we came for but we were mainly there to get his ass out of the escort game. He had token two of our women and they disappeared off the face of earth. Like where was he taking them? Well that bust went well it was the first bust that got James recognized by the FBI. It looked as if we were on a vacation shopping and ran into a little trouble at a hotel.

“the rules here are different if he annoys her enough shell smack him babe.” He said kissing my left cheek.

“mmmm mmmm, that’s not okay.” I was looking back at the child and mom. And just like that, whoop. She smacked the yelling child over the head and he stood straight up walking behind her.

“wow, she totally did what you said she would.” I turned back to James. Now when I think about it, his eyes were glowing. He was smiling at me, “your so nosy, get out their kool aid girl.”

I smiled to myself, “maam, weve landed, you can grab your carry ons and exit.” I was flying coach, I could afford it.

Outside I finally caught me a cab and gave the man the address to log into his gps. I fixed myself up in a mirror I had with my make up pack.

“You look beautiful.” The driver said looking through the rear view mirror at me. I looked up at him, kinda smiling but sort of not because I forgotten how creepy Portland cab drivers were.

“Thanks.” I put my things away looking at the meter which read $8.00 already. Damn I should of got a rental.

10 mins later, the meter read 64.25 and I told him stop it I would be just a minute. I hopped out the cab, and jogged up toward the house and rung the door bell. No one answered, I rung it again. An elder woman who looked to be about 78 answered, she was white of course. Gray hair, glasses, old wrinkled skin, but her nails were done. Red, blood red, and she had a look that ‘She don’t play no games’. “Hey, im Cynthia, I think I spoke with you yesterday on the phone?” she looked me up and down. Looked around to see if anyone was with me, “wheres the child?” tht caught me completely off guard and I didn’t know what to say.

“Uhhh.”

Chapter 8

"Come in." she opened the door up completely and moving aside to let me in. I walked in and stopped at what looked like an intersection. The left went to the dining room the right to the living room and forward was a hallway and a stair case.

Click

"Who sent you." When I turned around she had a black and brown shot gun pointed toward my head. What the heck had I gotten myself into?! I dropped my purse and everything in it. I didn't have a gun, I didn't really think I needed one. I thought I was dealing with an old ass woman. Then again she had a house full of convicts.

"Im here for Romel, im his brothers wife, I swear! No one sent me no one im family his brother has been murdered and I want to find out who did it." my hands were up.

She walked toward me studying me. This was the scratchy voice old woman, wow this was really crazy. An old woman with a SHOT GUN pointed at my head. i didn't know what to do how to react was this a dream? Was James worth this shit? Yes he was, but he wasn't.

"how the fuck do you know Romel has a twin brother? And where is the piece of shit really?" She asked pushing the gun into my left cheek. I was scared, so scared I almost peed my pants but you know what. I came for answers and that's what I was gone get.

"Look maam."

"my names Nann." She put more pressure on it. She was about 5'7" pretty tall right? Pretty dang strong too.

"Look nann, I told you who I am, and what I was here for. I didn't come all the way here to fight, I came to find my mans killer. I know he can help me, hes the only one who can help me. Please nann, I just need to talk to him." I begged her. I damn near cried. She let the gun down for a second than let it back up.

"hes not here, you can wait for him here though, don't touch anything don't talk to anyone, don't go anywhere. You disobey me I will shoot you." It looked to be an ordinary house, but it was a half way house. I guess she was the officer or something that owned it. she walked off and I walked toward the door, "I have to tell the driver im staying." I said grabbing at the door knob. I heard the gun cock again.

"I'll have someone go out there and get it how many bags you got?" she asked.

I scoffed, "1 I didn't plan on staying long, I wanted to get the information I needed and leave." I let the door knob go, looking back at her. She yelled for someone to go and escort me the cab driver thought nothing of it as I paid him.

Walking through the house it looked like a regular ass house but it couldn't have been. She escorted me to a room and left me there.

"So you know about Ramone?" I asked her sitting on the bed.

"Hes a voodoo practicing bitch, whose always been obsessed with pimping. Im surprised he married you, you don't look his type." She looked me up and down.

I was almost offended by that, "and what is his type?"

"a pretty face, nice body, and a quiet mouth, you look a little too flashy and your nosy. You looked Romel up, therefore you digged deep. I suggest you watch your ass miss Cynthia, you don't know shit about the man you married." She slammed the door close leaving me clueless. Was I kidnapped again?! What in the world man. I can't believe this.

I sat there hours going by, deciding to take a nap. My phone was ringing, I looked over at it at the other side of the twin bed and grabbed it. It read my mother's name, she really thought I was gone answer for her. i ignored it, and jumped at the sight of a black figure staring at me at the end of my bed.

"So my brother sent a chick to kill me?" a male's voice I've heard before spoke. "I'm just wondering how long he plans on faking dead before you try to pop me and come out the cuts." He said chuckling. "You know hes really a slick sick ass dude im surprised dude aint the walking dead somewhere." His hands were in the position like he was playing a piano but with a 9 mm in his left hand.

"I don't want to kill you, I just want some answers."

"ANSWERS?" I sat up on the bed reaching for the light switch on the lamp on my left side.

WOW whatre you talking about, you travel all the way from Georgia, with papers on me." He ossed the papers at me. I could see clearly he was UNOS twin. He looked every bit of him, I felt ke I was looking a ghost dead in the face.

HELLO?!" he walked around the bed coming toward me.

Its just you.."

Just me what?!" he stopped inches from my face. "I cant be having this kinda heat. I got to get ny shit back right I cant be having the feds not even fake ones." He froze after saying fake ones nd sat back facing the door on the edge of the bed.

im not with the law enforcement I swear I swear. I just want to know why uno kept you a ecret." I scrunched my eyes up trying to fix out what he was going to do next.

Is that why you came De'Aytra."He didn't turn back to look at me.

mooth, he called me by my real name, letting me know he went through all my things.

Your brother was involved in a big ass escort operation. My boyfriend was an accomplice, we obbed we killed we sold females we made money. My boyfriend just got hired by the FBI and noney was coming in even more after he did. His father was help but he later fell out when nings got serious."

What does any of this have to do with you coming to find me?" he looked over his right noulder back at me.

Your brother was murdered also."

Do you know my brother stole 50,000 and 200,000 worth of cocaine from me? We stashed it ogether, was suppose to go down together. But I always knew he was on some weird shit. Too motional for my type of business anyways, bitch ass nigga sent me to jail you know that? He old his soul to the devil along time ago ma, he aint dead."

why does everybody keep saying that? If theres something I need to know please tell me."

e was definitely different from Uno just by the way he spoke and I could feel his words were ist bold and you could tell he was serious without looking him in his face. It was just like, I on't know how to explain it. But I was feeling him a little bit, is that weird?

don't know why you even came here."

"I came because I need to find out who killed my man and give them some payback, I owe that to him."

"And who's going to pay me back huh?" he finally turned his head to the right looking at me from the corner of his eye.

My head was going crazy with ideas at this point of how I could get 250,000. I had 22,000 stashed but I wasn't going to touch that just yet.

"I have rich parents. I can supply you with the money." I suggested.

"Under what condition?"

"Your help."

"I never pass up money. "He said walking out of the door and closing it behind him.

Cynthia

Itd been days being in the hole. I didn't see the sunlight, I hadn't showered, and I hadn't made a phone call. All I wanted to do was talk to my baby Romney. Every night in this hell hole I dreamt of the day I had her. The way she looked at me and how pretty she was. She was 7lbs 7 ounces. Who could forget those numbers? My lucky number 7. She was born on the 7th of the 7th month, at 7:07 a.m.

I was so sick to my stomach and my head spun every time I thought about throwing up, which was every second. I gagged at the smell and the seriousness of my situation.

"I just want my daughter." Tears started flowing, they just wouldn't stop even after praying I felt helpless. I couldn't help my daughter. U couldn't help myself and no one was going to help me.

More and more days had gone by and all I was receiving was gross ass plastic plates Of garbage they called food. Like I was really gone eat that. Ill starve before I gain a bunch of jail fat that won't go anywhere when I get out. Which was the thing, I didn't know if I was getting out or not.

My trial was real soon, I forgot how many days id been here so it might've been today tomorrow, next week im not sure I really didn't care. Wasn't like id see Romney or Detra there

No one was on my team, I didn't have the time to reach out to anyone so it was all hopeless wishing theyd come.

That steel door had made a sound, like someone was opening it. it was a dull light with a man standing in the door way.

"Cynthia Cynthia Cynthia, miss diddy girl." he said coming near me than squatting to get a look at my face.

"You been in here since I last seen you?" he said grabbing my chin causing me to look him in the eye. I snatched away with all the little energy I had left. I wasn't eating so I was worn out, thirsty, stinky, my lips were crusty and id been picking at them forever.

I managed to snatch away with the little energy I had left in me, and it wasn't much of that since I hadn't been eating.

"don't flatter yourself, you look like shit." he said lifting over me. "You know Romney came with your foster mother to visit you today."

"Romney?" I couldn't believe my ears. My baby came to see me. my whole everything lit up and I didn't even think of if she was here or not.

"you wanna see Romney?" he asked. I nodded, he didn't know how bad I wanted to see and hold her. I wanted to smell her so bad, just smelling her would of made my days in here just better.

"If you want to see your daughter Cynthia, your going to have to talk."

I was ready to fucking sing to see my baby.

Chapter 9

Desire Styles

I was on my way with Lindsay to meet Diamond at Chocolate Sity, a club Diamond went back to after Uno's death and Diddy being taken into custody she really didn't have much of a choice. The crazy part was the money she was making at the club was still going into Diddy and Uno fagget ass pockets. This dumb broad didn't save any money, none of us thought to do that though. Lindsay had been still making her money posting, while I just did hair. I was messing with some kid who said he was gone be the next big drug lord, knowing damn well he was just on powder, talking, he was really on that scarface shit, and that shit right there it wasn't cool at all. Nothing about scarface was ever cool to me. why did men look up to a coke head who ended up murdering his sister and basically committing suicide because he thought he was invincible.

I Diamond and Lindsay had been rocking tough since Uno died though. They paid me to do their hair and makeup when they had plays and when diamond went in to work, which was like everyday. Diamond said working was fun, shed been taking pole dancing classes for the past week and swore she was just a big ass pole dancer. It was crazy we all had been hanging out because when Uno was here it seemed like everyone tried to impress him too much. Everything we did for eachother was really to get him to notice us. But now since he was gone, we all shined. We didn't really need him, I mean, I didn't. I had customers hair to do. Bitches from the club, drug dealers, I even retwisted a cousin of futures hair and he told me he was gone introduce me. did you see Monica's hair cut in the black beauty February's addition? Yeah baby, I did that. Mothafuckas thought I wasn't gone be shit but look at them! Dead and in jail. Sad to say but oh well, that hoe thought she was so much better than me. Than had the nerve to call me and ask to take care of her baby! Oh my gosh too funny, funny how karma works. It worked in my favor, but I wasn't going to let Romney suffer because her momma was a punk wanna be ass bitch. Her daddy too shit, they owned a whole beauty salon and didn't put me in that to work, instead im fucking sucking and getting ran through. That's not fucked up its passed fucked up matter a fact, I think I fuck got tired of me and moved on.

"its so funny shes in jail." I spoke out loud driving down MLK. LINDSAY looked over at me with a lost face.

"bitch who?!" she asked loudly. "Drew aint in jail is he?" she was talking about the lil dude I messed with. They called him Drew, of course his real name was Andrew. He was a lil hot head, his name on facebook was Drew Monatanna Gunnin . just the absolute most, it was funny but it wasn't Diddy in jail funny.

"Girl no, his lil ass gone be in juvie if anything. Shit he needa go so I can empty out the safe he got at his momma house."

Lindsay busted out laughing covering her mouth. Her nails were a hIGH lighter pink, which I was gone steal the color next but I only mentioned it because they were bomb. "he does not live with his momma."

"You right, but I rather him live with her than be shacked up at a base head house paying her damn bills and shit just to turn her joint into a trap."

Lindsay shook her head and smacked on her gum, "girl that's how them trapping ass niggas be I told yo ass." I looked at her from the corner of my eye.

"you kill me dude." I said laughing along with her.

"No im so foreal, but who you talking about Diddy?"

"Yeah girl, has she called you?" I asked.

"Hell naw, she aint gone call my white ass, as much shade as I threw. I wouldn't call me either, shit I know what happen is fucked up . I don't think shed kill Uno tho."

"why?" I snapped.

"Fuck you mad for bitch?" she busted out laughing again.

"Im not mad, I just think why wouldn't she kill him? She wanted to run shit." I knew deep down in my heart she didn't kill him but I didn't want that bitch out. If she got out on GOD id murk that hoe. That's just how much I couldn't stand the bitch.

We had just pulled up to the club and was on our way in.

"I should be a dancer huh?" Lindsay said twerking to nothing as we walked through the parking lot.

"Bitch no." we laughed in unison. I was really growing on Lindsay, she was a bad white bitch and she knew it.

But today we linked for one thing, MONEY. We needed to put our pretty little heads together and think of a plan. I wanted to move to Africa and they had plans too. I mean I wasn't starving or anything I just wanted to move around, staying In Georgia only had me locally famous. Traveling with Uno and Diddy only made us famous to the clients but here we are now no clients no money back to our hustling ways. I bet you diddy had everything she needed in jail shit the bitch might've started selling drugs or even pussy to the guards by now. Shit you know they say once a hoe always a hoe, we rely on our pussy to get every job done. I BET IT WORKED THOOUGH!!!! Hoodrat .

Getting inside free wasn't a problem, the Bouncer knew who we were, and who we were coming to see.

"So sorry about Uno ladies. Bottle on me, okay? Tell Diamond get Spike to send one of choice." The bouncer politely let us in.

"We don't need a sympathy bottle baby, we got it." I said rolling my eyes. I wasn't one of Uno's girls anymore and people needed to get that.

Lindsay hit my arm, "shit ill take the sympathy bottle, turn up! Lets get chocolate wasted!" she screamed running inside. I laughed following after.

Even though it was early, about 2 in the afternoon the club was packed. Money was being tossed and ass was shaking. I spotted Diamond giving a table dance to a group of gentlemen and had to come get her attention.

She seen me and hopped off the table collecting her money; heading to the back. Lindsay was located at the bar chopping it up with a few dudes attention she had grabbed coming in.

I was just trying to find a table in a corner that wasn't around the loud music. After about 10 minutes of searching I found the perfect one. I flagged down Lindsay and Diamond while ordering us some drinks and they met me back at the table ready to talk.

"Lets toast yall." Lindsay was drunk already, I could see it and diamond could too. "Yo drunk ass." Diamond said rolling her eyes. "You only been here 20 mins lind, really?"

"what the hell everybody mad about?!" she asked sucking her teeth.

"Girl we here to talk money. I aint trying to shake my ass and sweat all day." Diamond said putting her hair into a bun.

"you sweat when you fuck." Lindsay laughed sipping her drink.

Do you ever be serious?" diamond rolled her eyes.

I live." Lindsay took another sip.

and I work hard." Diamond slammed her hands onto the table.

mad or nah." Lindsay laughed, "if you work hard youd be rich by now." The two just kept ickering at eachother until I said what I have been thinking about for weeks.

m thinking about taking Romney from her mother."

the FOSTER momma?" Lindsay looked at me like I was insane, and she was so fucking right.

Hell yea."

Bitch what? How the fuck is we suppose to get some money doing that?"

We kidnap her silly, hold her for ransom."

Okay and when she goes back? what if the police find out?"

We tell her no police or we kill the little bitch." Lindsay blurred out.

Hold on now watch your mouth." I said looking at her in disgust,

That drunk shit gone get you slapped." Diamond laughed.

By who?! Desire? I aint worried." Lindsay took another sip of her drink. I ignored her. white rls tended to talk a lot when they were drunk.

can we be serious about this shit?! This little girl knows our faces, she knows you like the back f her hand desire. Na huh this shit aint gone work, my damn freedom on the line." Diamond pped her drink showing she was nervous.

well youll be in here twerking yo happy broke ass on, cus after a minute diamond you wont be oppin. Not when theirs bitches who look like Lindsay willing to shake for free. No offense nd."

had to give it to her straight. No one else would, so I sure did.

Plus you act like what we was doing before was legal." Lindsay added, that's why I loved this hite girl she was so with the shit.

“That’s Uno’s daughter, do you have no loyalty?” Diamond was really trying to argue wit me about it.

“diamond, I have been nothing but loyal to this mothafucka so much I LOST money and took ass whoopings for Diddy when she was still fucking tricks!”

Both the two mouths dropped, they didn’t know Diddy had been still tricking, no one but me knew. Did I tell a soul? No. I kept my mouth shut and chopped that shit to the game, shit I knew she needed to keep her hustle right in order to pay me for them hair do’s I did for her and Romney.

“Well, I guess the bitch wasn’t perfect.” Lindsay broke the silence.

“Look, I don’t know what you got against Diddy, but how is this gone work. Like really we don’t have no type of plan.”

“Diamond, just shut the fuck up and listen. You acting real pussy AND I aint got time fuh it fuhrea’.” She was bringing the country out of me and I hated to get country.

“So this how this one down play, the foster mother is a doctor, Rom goes to work with her. But will be in the childrens play room, we dress as nurses. We can always get scrubs from Ross, Citi Trendz or something. We get in and out, Diamond since you pissy pussy over there pissing yo’self you will sit at the front chatting it up distracting...”

“wait, im too fine to work in a hospital they gone know something up.” Lindsay and I cut our eyes at this dumb ass girl.

“And I thought I was a dumb white bitch, will you shut that dumb shit up.” I high fived Lindsay and we laughed in unison at this dumb broad.

“Okay, serious shit tho, bruh. Im READY. We can really do this you know that?” I was so sure we could. So many people snatched babies from the hospital all the time and security at Grady wasn’t gone be all that tight so I know we was gone get this shit in.

“Tonight.” Lindsay raised her cup waiting for us to join.

“Tonight bitch.” I toasted with her. We looked to Diamond who had her arms crossed and was pouting.

“Tonight, but I swear if we get caught. Yall hoes betta bail out cause I got me.” she finally toasted smiling

“We aint got to worry about the law, I got somebody on the inside.”

“Since when?” Diamond asked.

“Since officers pay for pussy, duh. Yall telling me yall aint never had a officer trick on you?”

“he must not be a low budget ranking Desire, aint no officer gone help us get away with kidnap?”

“This one will, im helping him out and hell help me out. He owes me this.” I was trusting in him after what I did to help me out with his every day stressful life.

“I actually love you crazy bitches.” She added as we toasted and all gulped our drinks.

Hours had gone by and I was ready to hit this lick and get it over with Romney knew who I was so it would be easy to get her to come along with me. Lindsay was with Diamond and they were in position all I had to do was get Romney. No one questioned us no one, not even security talk about dumb ass country people. Didn’t care to question a bunch of sexy bitches in a hospital full of foreigners, they knew damn well we didn’t belong but I guess easier for me.

I had to get the bitch at the kids desk to get away fast and she didn’t want to go nowhere. It was really difficult and I hated to do it but I hit that bitch over the head with my heels. It was so funny to see her flop. I dropped the clipboard over the desk and bloop, heel right over her head. It wasn’t a lot of blood and I was so nervous because I could’ve sworn the hospital had cameras, but I guess they didn’t huh.

Now I was sitting at a desk where the kids came in and out, mothers signing them in and out asking about this damn Cerena bitch and I told a different lie every time. Like damn this bitch must be famous or something it’s a new better looking bitch at the counter, forget about her. I played with a pen twirling in the chair wondering where the fuck was Romney and this old stubborn bitch already. The phone rang, it probably was diamond scary ass she was calling every second,

“what diamond I know this you.”

“Um, no sorry I was calling to speak with my OBGYN.”

“Oh im sorry you got the wrong line maam.”

“well can you connect me to them?”

“Um, im sorry I don’t know their exstention.” I rolled my eyes.

“are you around somebody that do?”

“Look bitch I said I don’t know you holding my line up.” I slammed the phone down. People here get on my damn nerves I swear, like know who the fuck you calling. really wasn’t mad at her she wasn’t THAT rude or nothing I was just irritated this bitch hadn’t brought Romney in yet. Like it was already going on 8 p.m. when did the bitch come in?!

“you must be new?” I heard a familiar voice ask. I looked up to the foster mom and Romney in her arms sleeping.

“Oh im sorry you heard that, please don’t report me I just started and I didn’t know people could be so cruel over the phone,”

“Right, well you should work on your skills there are children who stay in here. Im going to go lay her down shes had a long day.”

“Ill actually lay her down for you, here.” I reached for coming around the desk. She gave me a funny look that read bitch please.

“Ill lay her down myself, so do you know what happen to Cerena, shes usually the one in here with the kids. She loves her job wouldn’t imagine them to replace her.” This bitch was itching.

“Do you have somewhere you need to be, I sent her to go get the kids some snacks that’s where she is, nothing has changed.”

The lady turned back to me and than kept moving forward, she was getting suspicious and I was getting anxious. If I had to knock this stupid ass bitch out I would, it wasn’t like she could see my face I had a mask over it. If anybody asked I didn’t want to get sick. It wasn’t illegal to wear these things.

She finally got to a couch in the back room and laid Romney down, I didn’t take my eyes off her.

“You know your not suppose to leave the front desk just in case someone comes in.” she looked me up and down, “They let you wear heels in here?” I laughed to myself I was gone have to knock this bitch out and I was gone enjoy it because she was working nothing but my nerves.

“Has anyone ever told you how funny you are?” I asked taking my heels off.

“No don’t take them off I was just saying, it’s a little unusal, but its chilly in here I don’t want you sick your not wearing any socks.” I smiled and knodded gripping both my heels in my hands, soon as she turned around to kiss Romney I was going to fuck her up, “well, I should go im already late, please be safe and kind to these kids.” She brushed pass me without even looking back and just like that she left. For a minute I was hesitate of if she knew what I was going to do or she was rushing to get to her floor. Anyways I had to move fast, I picked Romney up looking her in the face and kissing her forehead, “I missed you little girl.”

Chapter 10

DeAytra

I had been calling my moms phone for the past hour, she had sent me a text saying she couldn't find Romney, my foster sisters daughter. Luckily me and Romel were already on the way back. Like not even 5 hours ago we were at a half way house back in Portland negotiating prices for each others help. But as if right now im trying to figure out how in the actual fuck could you lose a child In that big ass hospital after hours?! Shes probably scared out her damn mind, and it's my entire fault for not taking her into custody.

"Theres nobody at these desks but a flock of fucking police outside searching for my niece perfect." I looked over a counter than grabbing at my face. The hospital wasn't even evacuated, it was people standing and sitting everywhere.

"by blood shes my niece so im next if kin, ill get everything her dad owes me." I looked back to Romel, who was smiling rubbing his hands together following behind me. The past few days I spent with him im not gone lie were actually not bad. He didn't pay me much attention, at least that's what I thought. I guess I wasn't his type either. Was James the only one who liked my long colorful nails and loud colored weave?

"since Uno was 1 , you must be Dos, like number 2? Shes been with me her whole damn life all that is mine, and im paying you anyways." I shook the thought of Romney losing everything.

"when you learn the back story itll be funny to you too. Handle your business im hitting a snack machine." All I seen was a flock of ugly depressed people who I soon would be solving cases for in my life time. I was offered a job with car and traffic injuries, money always came through in that department. But it wasn't big money.

Imagine this, your husband, in my case, James; the super intelligent detective who later goes to the FEDS catches bad guys. I can be the DA or just be the PROSECUTOR in the courts. That's where the money was getting paid by the state or even bigger. James was so big in my eyes. I knew I hit the jack pot with him.

My phone rang snapping me out my thoughts, "Mom? Where are you at?"

"Im 10 seconds from calling the FBI, that's where im at on this, its been almost 2 hours, I have security at all the doors." She sounded as if shed been crying and I almost felt sorry for her.

was standing there twirling in a circle really trying to figure out what in the hell had happen. nd for an odd moment I seen another person down the hall from me. We made eye contact, nat face was so familiar I screamed her name before i completely recognized her. "Desire!"

walked quickly toward her, and she turned her focus forward walking out the entrance of the ospital. By time I made it there she was gone. What was that about, I never did anything to nat girl?

brushed it off and made my way to the child care, where day care but at night was.

I don't know who she was, all I know is she's going to jail!" a lady was screaming from the ffice as I got closer. She was on a stretcher; I could imagine the pain she had because she was incing between every word, holding her head. My mom was helping her nurse it.

So what did you tell 12, what happen?"

Honey, you're not telling time, their called the police, and I told them the truth. I dropped omney off late and there was a hooker in heels working the counter. I said she was uspicious."

Mom a hooker?"

Yes a hookah." She added some slang to sass me. "I know what they look like De'Aytra, I raised ou to not be one."

And Im a lawyer."

Not yet your not."

I came to help find my niece."

the niece you wouldn't take before? Save the bull De'Aytra we went and seen Cynthia. Shes een calling you for weeks and you couldn't care to help her out with the only Grandchild that I o have?" she looked at me in disgust. My mother always reminded me of Claire from the bill osby show. She was so beautiful, with long natural hair. I just loved it. But right now she was nna make me slap the shit out her.

GIRL." Slipped out, "Im not getting involved with that shit, she knows damn well I told her she as going to end up hurting that man, you ever think maybe she killed em. That's on her, I elped enough, James is dead because of her and Ramone."

My mom waved me off walking out of the room.

“Don’t you walk away, whats going on with you taking up for her?”

“What do you mean DeAytra I owe it to her to have taken care of Romney. Cynthia has always did everything on her own, and I thought I was giving her tough love I thought I was being a fair parent because I made you do it and look how you turned out, an almost lawyer. Now my other child is in prison, her husband was murdered and every bodies too lazy to find the killer.”

“I lost my husband.”

“He wasn’t your husband, he was your boyfriend, and you didn’t have any children.”

There it was, how she felt about me and James. It was all fake to her, it didn’t mean anything because we didn’t have children or was married.

“Well he loved me.”

“Cynthia bought that house you live in didn’t she?”

“Oh come on she was dirty, mom, all that was ‘hookah’ money. Some was drug money; you know we all participated in this. You knew she didnt graduate, never got a loan to own them houses, and apartments, they muscled people.”

“Is this court, are you trying to convince me why you neglected your family? You accepted every penny you and that nigga lover.” She was referring to James.

“Wow, im i missing something?”

“I think your jealous.”

“Of what, Diddys In jail now, wheres her husband dead. And its because she killed him just like she killed mines.”

“That’s the bitch you were pretending to be when you came to my home.” Romel walked up catching us both off guard.

“Your alive?!” She backed into me.

“I never died.” He smiled showing off the most gorgeous set of white teeth. How had he been in prison so long with the perfect set of teeth?

“Aye ma I gotta holla at you.”

“ma?” my mom looked back at me.

“so what is this, you fake your death and run off with this whore and your daughter, wheres my grandbaby!” she got in his face. He was way different from Ramone.

“Mom, are you on drugs?” I grabbed her pulling her out his reach.

“That’s Ramone.” She pointed toward his face.

“Im definitely not that snitch ass nigga and if you get in my face one more time yelling ima punch you ugly.”

“I suggest you explain yourself right now.” My mom looked back to me. “if your not Ramone who are you and what the hell are you doing with Deaytra.”

“Hes not Uno mom, he’s a twin.”

“Ramone was an only child. He wouldn’t lie to me, he was...”

“Playing us all.” I added.

“Can we go?” He looked at me and licked his lips in the sexiest way, I don’t know if it was intentionally or not but lord my body caught a chill.

My mother was in a moment of shock until I felt a sharp sting to the face, “you brought him here and now Romney is gone. You believe your sister murdered him now?!” My mother looked at me.

“I don’t know what you plan on doing with him, but you are sick, you are disgusting. Don’t ever show your face around me ever.” She screamed. She looked Romel in his eyes, “you find my grand baby or ill pay the best lawyer I can find, even if I have to bring Al back to life you mothafuckas better pray.” She gave me one last look before storming off.

With rage in my eyes i took off to the nearest exit.

“aye, im trying to tell you something.” Romel caught up to me grabbing my arm.

We were almost to my car I had parked in the hospital parking lot.

“Im sorry.” I apologized. “my family isn’t usually broken like that. Shes just stressed out about Romney and Cynthia being in jail.”

“I don’t care nothing about your fucked up family. Did Cynthia kill my brother?”

I looked down at my keys and let out a deep breath, “the truth? I don’t know.” I looked him into his eyes.

“that hate you got about a white boy aint even that serious foreal like. I mean it aint my business but I got blood in this.”

“what you mean?”

“I saw the kid, she looked like she called me daddy. I couldn’t tell at first if she was looking at me than she kind of ran toward me. She was with some bitch who looked like she was way too fine to be working up in here.” He pointed to the hospital.

Chapter 11

Cynthia

"So you ready to talk?" a bailiff chuckled into my ear. "that was easy."

"im not talking because one of yall tried to kill me. Ima see my daughter today that's the only thing keeping my heart beating."

"the pretty fat one?"

"shes not fat asshole."

"naw she a little fat guh, I seen her. Shes cute though, don't be mad . she just fed right."

I rolled my eyes, and fixed my hair. I had slicked it back with water, and was ready to see my little biscuit. I hate she had to see me like this.

The door swung open to where they said she was. There her and my mama was. I instantly ran to her crying. My foster mom had tears also.

"Mama." I reached for a hug and she gave me the tightest hug shed ever given me.

I sat there with Romney in my lap asking 21 questions about what shed been doing, and what mama had her doing, and how she felt about me being away so long.

"Cynthia we need to talk." Mama reached for my hands. I patted Romney on the rump so she knew it was time for grown folks to talk. She sat on the ground playing with the available toys.

"I didn't kill him." I started it off.

"I know you didn't,I know you loved him. The day of the wedding was the happiest day of your life. Now murder, 3 counts, I raised you better."

"DeAytra wont help. I knew you were busy and im so sorry I know you love your career and you and pops living it big. Take her please, im not getting out of here. I know im not, im going to court next week. Im going to see that the jury only tries me for soliciting women, and probably a few robberies and racketeering. Im sorry mama. I really am. I didn't mean for all this to happen" I bursted into tears.

"Ill see it I do better with this one than I did with you two. Because yall family, you took care of DeAytra when she was off following behind some country ass white boy when she should've stayed in them books became a doctor like her mother, and not a lying stack off law books like her father." I could hear the rage in her voice at DeAytra.

"I will do it, I love you. I shouldn't have been so tough."

"Its okay Grandma, mommies coming with us. Romney grabbed our hands, "Lets go now im bored."

"Im staying baby, I live here now. Go with granny and wait for me okay? Hopefully I can beat these murder charges and come home to you in a few months."

Looking into my daughters eyes I could tell she didn't know what I was talking about but she knew I wasn't leaving with her and it hurt her. Her lip began to poke out and she buried her face into my chest.

"Im sorry baby."

"is it because daddy died?"

The door swung open, "Time to go."

"Please a little more, please, please." I begged as they came in escorting them away.

I sat there for almost 2 hours before the detective I been speaking to the last month had come in.

"we had a deal."

The detective came in and sat down.

"Need a cigarette, need anything?" he asked smiling at me.

"I need a good ass lawyer." I answered wiping my tears away.

"Yeah, no way your getting out of here, you're a crime boss, soliciting women, robberies, killings, drugs, racketeering and endangerment of a child."

"you say that the judge wont let me see her ever." I snapped.

"Well see that's the only leverage I have over you." He said smiling coming closer.

"What do you want please don't hurt my baby." I begged dropping to my knees.

Whatever you want, please, whatever you want." I was ready to kiss this man shoes.

is phone was vibrating like crazy and he had looked at it a few times. His eyes rolling at who as calling.

excuse me Cynthia I have matters to take care of. Something that might pertain to your aughter. You want her safe? Take the rap for the 3 murders." He said getting up from his seat nd walking toward the door, " ugh and get off the floor." He walked out and my heart ropped.

Chapter 12

Desire

"Oh my fucking GOD! Oh My Fucking GOD!!! WHAT THE FUCK!" I shouted at the top of my lungs. Romney was in the other room watching cartoons and the girls had joined me in the front room. My boyfriend Drew had moved me into some little on the cabin in the woods house. I really didn't like it since my neighbors were about an 30 min run away. He thinks I don't know but he used to bring people out here and torture them with his friends. These kids from the hood is foreal sick these days but he was somebody little do boy who got treated like he was a prince, and treated me like a queen. I aint mad, keep it up baby I need you right now. Just a few more weeks nobody in this damn world will know I even existed. New everything baby, hair, name, game, and profession.

In case you wondering where my house? Man Since uno had died in the middle of my payments the house was no longer mines or his; he put Romney on the deed. Everything was in her name from diddy to all of Uno's possessions. The crazy part about this is the house was token, its all under investigation. Uno is like I guess a big deal. Like the empire we helped him build got him caught up to a point if I don't act like a victim I could go to jail for prostitution, robbery, murder The list goes on, I helped GOD I helped with all that stupid shit.

"Yo Chill that yelling shit out and tell us was sup, you seem spooked." Diamond was sittin on the ledge of my couch moving her hands as she talked. She sounded so irritated it was getting me angry. Her New York accent was really bugging me because I think she had an attitude with me and I don't like bitches with attitudes.

"Yeah like yo ass seen a ghost or something." Lindsay sat on the bar stool opening a bag of chips.

"I did, Uno was at the hospital he seen me, he seen me and didn't say anything. He looked me dead in the face and Romney called him daddy and he was confused like. That's why I had diamond meet me and take her out the east exit. I have never been so shooken in my life. I thought he was dead." I was walking back and forth scared out of my mind.

"are you serious?" diamond screamed.

"YO STOP YELLING! The kids in the room, have you hoes no class."

We gave Lindsay the evil eye, “Bitch is you dumb? We’re going to fucking die now that he knows.” Diamond sucked her teeth crossing her arms and stomped her foot.

“no no no I thought he was dead?” I asked looking at Lindsay.

“Girl im just as shocked as you, I aint heard from nobody in months.”

“Okay, I gotta make a call to my guy. Yall hoes bounce, ill call yall when I get some answers.”

“you better get some fucking answers Styles, because if I wake up dead.” Diamond had her finger pointing in my face.

“you cant wake up dead.” I said pushing her out the door.

“Well I aint worried as long as I get paid, he didn’t do shit there so.”

“you know that’s that same attitude got your teeth kicked in, you remember that shit? Yeah wasn’t okay imagine what hes going to now he knows we took his kid.” Diamond said walking off to her car.

“I shouldn’t of agreed to this shit, so fucking stupid.”

“so you don’t want your cut?” I shouted to her.

She raised her middle finger pulling out in her fully paid off cherry red Charger ’16.

“I don’t really care, aye Die gimme a ride.” Lindsay walked up on Diamonds charger.

Diamond sucked her teeth and rolled her eyes “ask her you could use her accord?”

“bitch I aint finna be seen in no Honda, I got 2 thou-wows worth of heels on, I WILL WALK Fatima!” She yelled Diamonds real name hoping into the car and waving bye.

I closed the door, and looked for my phone. I dialed this man number 10 times before I got an answer,

“What desire, I was in an important meeting with a suspect.”

“I thought you said Ramone was dead?” I asked closing the bathroom door speaking just barely over a whisper.

“He is dead, whatre you talkin about? I was on scene to confirm his death and the other 2 victims.”

"look I don't care about your bitch and maybe baby. I did what you told. I want my money and I want these two bitches in jail with that bitch also."

"I thought you trusted them?"

"I don't trust diamond, shes getting really scared and shit because I seen a nigga look just like fuckin Uno today at the hospital. Explain that!"

He sat on the phone silent,

"No way hes alive, she shot him more than once… out of rage."

"Come on, get her to confess about something, we got her baby break her. I need my money tho, and I need them to not attend if you want me to go to court."

"she did want to take this to a jury but shes not going to win with you and some chick by the name Goddeua…"

Soon as I heard the name the face popped into my name. the girl raised in the church. Short pretty Hispanic Aztecan im not sure what she was. She was from Tiajuano that's where she had been picked up she been through hell out there with them guys. I guess she found herself back in the church. She used to tell us good stories, sounded like she was a damn warrior or something what she been through. But I felt like what she been through was the same as anyone else I mean, she ended up with us in the same position. She wasn't so special just because she could talk Spanish. She wasn't all that she was an average height, around 5'6" dark tan skin she used to rub this musky smelly dirt stuff she made on her forehead making a cross. Weird right? She was totally out of line but Uno said that's what he liked about her she was different and it was in her eyes. her soft eyes with silver lining. She almost looked like a baby, which I found creepy; if any man wanted her they were a pervert I mean the kid looked 15, a 15 year old who started fucking at the age of 11 or something.

"I thought she was in back in Mexico with the church or something?" I stumbled over my words just a little bit. I mean I didn't really care, but I had a right to know.

"she said her calling was to come back and help deliver justice to ones who once caused her pain. "

"so what does that mean? What does that have to do with her?"

"Don't dig too deep into someone elses situation, shes ready to confess. Shes ready to give up. I will have my little pay back and you will to. You want cash?"

I could feel a smile wipe across my face, "what about the hospital incident?"

"we get this show rolling, I got a judge on the case, we bump up the court to this Wednesday, and shes in Friday, along with your friends."

"How are you going to get them?" I asked.

"Set them up after the trial, they'll be wondering why you got on the stand and try you."

I knew what he was saying was true, but what was he going to do about the look alike out there.

"Ill handle everything else, trust me."

"you say It like you're the best." I giggle. I could feel a smile come across his face.

"Look, ill come by later."

I tried to reply but he hung up like he was stopping himself for falling for me. I guess this plan he had wasn't necessarily for me. I was just a pawn in his chess game. I sat on my toilet with my phone in my hand thinking like, was I going to really get away with this and if I do, LORD HELP ME!

I got up from the toilet opening the bathroom door peeking out to see if Romney had come out, she was occupied by something so that was fine by me. I took a huge breath of relieve. "the hard part is over now we wait."

Chapter 13

DeAytra

"So your moms not in any shape to loan you some money miss lady. I thought you said your parents were rich?" I watched Dos, I was gone start calling him that it seemed like the name irritated him enough; he was walking across my living room to the bar next to the balcony.

"Well, Dos. It doesn't look like we starving do it?"

"Was that thanks to my brother or your moms salary?" he poured him a double shot of Disaronno.

"My mother has always spoiled me; I never needed your brother that was my dumb ass sister thinking she knew what she was doing. She told me it was about the money and got caught up now shes in jail for his murder and recently we discovered the mistress was also pregnant. I told her about them the first time I witnessed it but he got the chick pregnant."

I felt my sisters pain, but killing uno and the girl only made her situation 10 times worse. She knew damn well she needed a hit or something; it's just since James murder we were all already being looked at and questioned. It was a cold case, nothing no one spoke so it was nothing I could do plus it being in another county, no one really cared.

"You know, I don't even know the girl but I think shes innocent."

My head jerked toward him. "Why?"

"If she loved my brother like you love James. Shes innocent."

"But shes not."

"You sound like you want her in jail."

"I-I-I really don't know at this point, with Romney...." I stopped in my sentence.

"The girl was light skin pretty curls, soft eyes, long legs, and her ass was sitting up in her scrubs." He laughed to himself.

"whats funny? That bitch kidnapped my niece." He took another shot and looked toward me.

haven't drunk alcohol in a long time. Its real good." He looked over the glass. I could see his yes glossing.

:hat little girl looks just like me." He laughed again. "I want her." He looked me over, "if she is ıy blood and Cynthia is innocent I want them, both."

could feel jealousy take over me, he didn't even know Cynthia and here he was ready to ride ɔr her.

So what if she is, what lawyer ..."

You lawyer. You want my help, you get her out." I was speechless. That wasn't apart of the lan.

she couldn't have killed him if someone has kidnapped her daughter." He added. And he was ght, I should of known that.

But how can I prove that in court, im not even licensed yet."

tll take time, but I got a plan. And if my brother loves your sister, hell show up soon enough nd when he does, ill have his bitch." He chuckled to himself, it was a little evil. But I wasn't oing to question it, he knew for a fact how I could find the dudes who did what they did to mes. He said he knew who'd put the hit out on Uno, we had had this conversation back in ortland.

'd been a week since Romney was missing, I had no clue what to do but hustle someone into etting me into their Law firm. Dos was on my ass about everything, he made sure he found out ow to get a visit in with Cynthia before her trial tomorrow and im nervous to actually see her.

you should be nervous, you denied your niece now sexy nurses have kidnapped her." He ughed.

your really an asshole, nice looking but a real dick."

probably why my brother fucked me huh?" he smiled showing off them beautiful teeth.

just want to meet her." I rolled my eyes as we walked into the prison where Cynthia was.

hecking in was easy the wait was long and aggravating. Im surprised she approved Romel ithout even seeing him, momma must of told her about him.

"Those visiting Cynthia, shes ready." The guard called out, and my heart sank. I have never been so nervous in my life.

I took a deep breath and walked into the visiting area with Romel patiently waiting to see Cynthia walk in.

I finally spotted her walking in, shed been in here for 2 months now and looked so different. Her hair was twisted and dangling pass her ears. Her ears were still big and chinky, her skin had broken out a little but she was so beautiful. I could see her face light up when she seen Romel. She couldn't have killed Ramone, id never seen her look so happy sad and angry all in one, it was breath taking.

"Ramone?" she said sitting down her voice cracking.

"Cynthia, its finally nice to meet the face to the name." he extended his hand over the table.

"Im so confused, Baby why are you, what happen, I seen you dead. Im so happy but I cant help but cry." Tears welled up in her eyes than she looked over to me, her whole everything went to rage.

"WHAT the fuck is this Ramone, you cheat you lie, you die, you come back and your with this bitch? Bitch give me 1 reason why I shouldn't bust yo head in this mothafucka after your disloyalty?" her voice was loud yet deep she meant every word she just asked me,

"MEYERS! Don't make us cut this visit short!" a guard yelled over to our table.

"No, were fine, sorry. Im here to help yo pathetic ass, this isn't your man, you should know that if you really knew your man, but too bad you don't." I couldn't help it, but to respond the way I did. I was so tired of this bitch thinking she was really better than me.

"Both of you chill the fuck out, listen here beautiful, I know your innocent." She looked back to Romel and her eyes went back to sadness.

"if your not ramone who are you and why are you here with her?"

"My names Romel, im sure your husband mentioned me, DOS." Shed heard the name before, her face expression indicated that.

"Ramone told me I could find you and you would help me. But he didn't tell me you.."

"Im his older brother by 3 minutes, I want you to come home you and romney."

"Romney is with my.."

“look, baby all that is irrelevant right now. I need you home.” He said looking her into her eyes. He was hypnotizing her, she was so struck.

“I go to court tomorrow, Goddeua and Desire are going to take the stand against me, my mom said shes got the best lawyer right now on the case.”

DESIRE? Soon as I heard that name I had a flashback seeing her scurry in a hurry out of the hospital.

“THAT BITCH!!!” I hopped out of my seat.

“That’s it! YOUR OUT OF HERE!”the guard rushed over to me, “Come on.” He grabbed my arm,

“Don’t touch me, I’m going, Cynthia I’m so sorry for your loss and blaming you for James murder.”

Itd been an hour before Romel returned to the car.

“shes beautiful, beautiful mind and all I can see why you so jealous.” He look s at me and smiles.

“Im not jealous, but I know who took Rom. This bitch is going down about my niece.”

We sped off.

Chapter 14

Desire

The face on them bitches Diamond and Lindsay face at the trial when they called me up there to stand against Diddy. I mean what the fuck could she do? The case was closed, that bitch was going down and she knew it. Now to let these hoes catch they self up, Diamond had been blowing my phone up.

Diamond – Bitch Is you serious!!

Tf we just did that hot shit and you get on the stand hello?

You snitch bitch.

Wait til I see you.

Its on and poppin hoe.

Lindsay – aye get back at me ,

wssup you being weird with ya white bitch.

I got to move this lil girl from my spot shit getting hot and tense especially since they convicted Diddy.

hello?

Diamond – I knew you was a snake bitch went to yo lil cabin in the woods hoe you moved all yo shit out wait til I catch you man

Lindsay – I spoke to diamond she said you moved yo stuff fr shorty?

Do us like that its been a few days no response wassup ma foreal

Me – YALL HOES quit texting me! Yall got that girl baby yall foul

Diamond – WHAT??? You set up ass bitch!!! Wait til I catch you hoe.

I know it was scandalous but oh well, I had been laying low for about a month I got my money, and I was on my way to get the fuck out of town, the easiest and quickiest way was the airport. When they asked me did I want protection, please, from who? All my enemies were locked up, and I planned to slay VEGAS! Yes bitch vegas Houston all that shit was finna get a new piece of me that wasn't my pussy.

An unfamiliar number was calling my phone probably was this bitch diamond shed been blowing me up since she was convicted for kidnap and assault on a nurse, yeah I kinda was wearing her tan YSL heels the night we kidnapped Romney. I guess I had shit more handled than I thought huh. I stuck my tongue out laughing and answering the phone.

I was now waiting to board the plane when the number called again,

"do you accept the charges.."

"blah blah blah..." I pressed 2.

"you fagget.."

"you still calling me in jail sweating me bitch its been a weeks serve yo 56 months"

"Wrong bitch, Desire, you should start listening. That was always your problem though, you was always running your mouth but ill be putting a fuckin foot in soon." The ended and I realized just who I was talking to. Cynthia, she said shed be seeing me soon, what the fuck was that about?

"Last call Desire Styles." I got up from my seat grabbing my carry on.

"Desire Styles?"

"Im fuckin coming can I get my fuckin bag?" I turned around to the same fuckin detective I used to fuck on. He had his badge out and cuffs ready,

"your under arrest for the kidnapping of Romney Meyers and aggravated assault with a deadly weapon.."
"are you fucking kidding me?" I screamed while someone grabbed my hands placing them behind my back.

"ill be putting a fuckin foot in soon" is all I heard in cynthias voice while they escorted me into the back of a police car.

Chapter 15

Cynthia

The day they convicted me foreal when that jury said guilty my whole heart dropped I was sentenced to life. I swear on my everything I would never kill my man, I love him. I looked at Deaytra she said shed help me and look at me. Romel said hed help me but look at me, finna be somebodies bitch. I cant win all fights, and I definitely couldn't beat these perverted ass guards up or keep them off of me.

I knew my life was over Romney wasn't there, my mom wasn't there, only person I seen was the bitches Diamond Lindsay Goddeua and punk ass Desire. I always knew Desire was a punk bitch but hearing Godduea do me like that after I had took her in when she was dying was horrible. the church had thrown her out, and banished her than. She was crying and begging me to take her in but i guess she hated my man, and took it out on me. Where was these hoes loyalty even my sister changed up on me. That shit was painful everybody hated me huh? What did I do but make these bitches pockets fat. They was out here fucking niggas for 50 60 bucks, maybe for free.

Funny thing was a couple days after trial, these hoes Lindsay and Diamond came strolling in. come to find out these bitches hated me way more than I thought. Diamond and Lindsay tried kidnapping my baby, now what could they possibly benefit from that. Money? Respect? Yeah Lindsay was released to her cell and I planned on paying her a little visit today. The devil has been talking to me lately and how im feeling, Lindsay will be my example for when they assign Diamond to her block.

My cell opened, it was time for count , I did as we are routine than headed toward C it was a level up from me. Lindsay knew I was coming, she had her hands in the air when I walked into her cell.

"Diddy I know you pissed but ..."

"But nothing bitch, what the fuck was you thinking?" I rushed her banging her head onto her top bunk.

She winced in pain but made no noise, "Please diddy, I didn't.."

"You didn't what?" I banged her head again, she dropped to knees. I kicked her in the face, she dropped and curled up into a ball. I just kept kicking and stomping her out. If there was anything I could fuck her up with in her cell Id hurt her worse than what she getting now. I wasn't strong enough, I wanted to make her scream.

"SCREAM BITCH!" I grabbed her hair , her head raised and I just sent so many blows to her face, and she let me. She knew what she had done, she knew this was the price to pay,

She stiffed up and all I know is she started shaking viciously but I couldn't stop hitting her. "fuck yo seizure bitch" I kept hitting her,

DIDDY! What the fuck, guard, somebody help." Her cell mate had returned and was screaming for someone) help. She pushed me off her, I fell sideways onto the toilet. Watching her shake made me even more mad, Die you white trifling bitch." My heart was full of rage.

hat dumb shit I had pulled was worth it to me, I spent another fucking month in the hole. But today I was etting out, and I was excited as fuck. Diamond would finally get to feel the rage I had in me.

/hen the guards let me free, I let a few hours kick in before I made my way to her. She was standing over ndsay who had a huge scar from stitches by her right eye. Im sure I did that, that's what that disloyal bitch ot, I always hated that bitch. She kissed unos ass a little too hard anyways. She spotted me and put her head own. Diamond made eye contact, her hair was in a high messy bun and she looked pissed as ever, and pale.

ne walked toward me, "You real bold bitch."

am from New York, look all that tough girl shit you need to hear this."

ll listen after I beat your ass." She smiled and shook her head.

Girl you cant whoop me, you may can beat Lindsay ass but who cant, now listen to what the fuck I got to tell ou. They got a warrant for Desires arrest, your sister found some evidence about our case."

Why would I give a fuck about?"

.ook we not innocent, I did help kidnap your daughter .." I moved closer to her but she kept her distance.

The detective that arrested you was fucking desire. They set you up." My whole heart dropped. I ran to a none. I had to get in touch with DeAytra.

Hey don't cut me." A bald headed bitch screamed to me when I took the phone before she could.

m doing life do you really wanna try me right now?" I gave her an evil look, the bitch knew to bow down.

dialed deaytra a few times no answer.

hey not answering." She said in my ear.

swear bitch you gone catch it today!" I turned to her.

Hello?"

) omg its so good to hear yo snake ass voice."

Diddy you are such a trouble maker you gave Lindsay a seizure?"

nd didn't stop whoopin the hoe til somebody got me off her." I laughed

hit like that aint gone help yo case."

“speaking of my case tell me something good bitch diamond said I was set up by the crooked bitch who arrested me.”

“It came up Marisol was his wife.” My mouth dropped.

“yes, hes dead tho.”

“wait what?” I screamed “he killed himself?”

“he went after romel thinking he was Uno and confessed everything. Marisol had been helping him close in on Uno and I guess she was in love with him too.” Hearing her say she loved him made me think of the what if’s.

“im scheduling you a hearing soon so be on your best behavior.”

“hearing you got your license?” this was all too exciting.

“yes romel..”

“romel ... ramones twin... where is he?”

“Hes in mexico... with Romney.. and Goddeua.”

“WHAT?!” I screamed.

“Its best for right now.”

“FOR WHO! You forgot she snitched on me.”

“YOU WANT your daughter caught up in a world you created seriously, start thinking about whats best for her. Shes with family, her real family.”

“She doesn’t know that man, you barely know him, whatchu fuckin him? I always knew you liked uno.”

“hes way different from that bitch uno ima let you know that right now. And if you want to come home suggest you tighten the fuck up. Its pay back time and you fucking it up. Ill be there within a few days. Act right.”

“is it true they have an arrest out for Desire?”

“yes, how about giving her a call, cant hurt your sentencing that bad.”

“sistah THAT’S THE BEST thang you said in months.” I hung up the phone and dialed Desires number she answered,

“you fagget..”

“you still calling me in jail sweating me bitch its been a weeks serve yo 56 months”

“Wrong bitch, Desire, you should start listening. That was always your problem though, you was always running your mouth but ill be putting a fuckin foot in soon.”

I looked back to diamond, “It aint over you next bitch.”

To Be Continued....

I just want to thank everyone who read this book. It takes a lot of imagination and dedication to write a book. With so many emotions and characters it's hard to separate reality and a book. To the young women and men out there ITS NOT ABOUT WHAT YOU KNOW, ITS WHO YOU KNOW!

Made in the USA
Monee, IL
08 November 2020